GUILTY OF LOVE

KACI LANE

Copyright © 2025 by Kaci Lane

All rights reserved.

This is a work of fiction. Names, characters, organizations, places, events and incidents are either products of the author's imagination or are used fictitiously. Any resemblance to actual persons, living or dead, or actual events is purely coincidental.

No part of this work may be reproduced, or stored in a retrieval system, or transmitted in any form by any means without written permission from the author.

*To everyone who has read all the Bama Boys and Apple Cart County Christmas books.
I finally finished Bradley's book!*

And especially for my friend Jillian, who was on an ARC break but agreed to fit in Bradley's story!

CHAPTER ONE

Bradley

"Hey, big dog. You're one good-looking son of a gun."

I lean away from the rearview mirror and slide on my sunglasses. Nothing like a little pep talk to keep me going.

Even though I'm running for reelection unopposed, there's a tiny fear that if I don't look, act, and sound heroic and confident at all times, I'll somehow lose.

I hop out of my Chevy and slam the door. One thing I did right first time around was not print a year on my political signs. The local printer was kind enough to add "re" in front of "elect" for a decent cost.

"Morning, Bradley."

I turn to Adrianne walking toward her salon.

"Morning, Mrs. Culp. Mind if I put one of these signs in the grass beside your shop?" I wave a sign above the truck bed for her to see.

"Not at all." She half smiles, then unlocks the side door to her building.

"Thanks," I call out as she goes inside.

I grab a rubber mallet and get to work. Her salon is in the middle of downtown—prime real estate. It's also a lot easier to spot than across the road at Paul's place. He has all sorts of junk parked out front and rarely weed-eats. It looks like a tornado hit a pigsty.

I stand to admire my sign and bump into something.

"Pardon me."

"Howdy, sir." I nod to a round fellow with rounder glasses.

He straightens the briefcase in his hand and pushes the glasses up the bridge of his nose. "Do you happen to know if Misty is here?"

I raise one brow. "She's still married to Woody, right?"

He looks a little too sophisticated for Misty's taste, but you never know with her.

"I just need to make sure she hasn't come to work yet."

I shrug. "Only one to come through was Adrianne."

"Thanks." He wipes his brow and continues to the front of the salon.

I watch him enter, then grab several signs from the bed of my truck. I'll put a few more in front of some storefronts down this row before moving toward the Pig, then the bank.

The good thing about a small town is it doesn't take long to cover downtown. The bad thing is I'll also need to put out signs on a lot of rural roads to attract attention.

Town starts to come alive as more people enter stores and open their doors to the public. I greet everyone and make it a point to ask the owners' permission before sticking any stakes in grass, even though the sidewalks are public property. It's just the gentlemanly thing to do.

When I'm down to one sign, I head for the bank. I

straighten my hat and smooth my shirt before going inside. I hope Ashley's up front for two reasons.

One: I don't like the man in charge here. At. All.

Two: I like her. A. Lot.

As luck would have it, I open the door to her beautiful blonde head. The sunlight trails from outside, outlining her form like a sexy angel.

I shake my head to keep from getting struck by lightning at that thought. Maybe angel wasn't the right comparison to use. I'll go with Taylor Swift in concert.

Yeah, lit up on stage in all her glory.

Her eyes shift from her computer screen as my boots hit the tile floor. Slowly her gaze meets mine, and she smiles. My cheeks involuntarily draw upward into what I imagine is a goofy grin.

She has that effect on me.

"Morning, ma'am." I tip the brim of my hat.

"Hello, Bradley. How can I help you?"

Let's see. You can give me your number, go to dinner with me, marry me . . .

"Can I stick my sign in your grass?"

She quirks a thin eyebrow upward as I raise the sign in my hand. "I'd be happy to help, but my grass isn't in this county."

I chuckle nervously. "I mean Samuel's grass." I clear my throat. This is sounding worse and worse. "Here on the bank lawn."

Her confusion slowly turns to a smile. She shrugs. "Fine by me. We are a public business."

"Thanks." I stare at her pretty blue eyes until they lower toward my hand.

Then I realize I'm still holding up the sign like an idiot at a protest. I slide my arm by my side, accidentally clipping the edge of her desk with the sign. A picture falls.

"I'm so sorry." I bend and pick it up.

"It's fine."

I lift my eyes to her leaning over the desk, her hand reaching for the photo. My fingers brush her tiny, manicured hand as she takes it from me. It's a photo of her with another pretty girl and a middle-aged couple.

"Is that your family?"

She nods. "Yeah, my parents and younger sister."

"You're the prettiest." I clamp my mouth shut. That was meant to stay a thought.

She quirks her mouth sideways as she adjusts the frame to where it was before.

"I mean, your sister is a very attractive woman as well, or girl. She looks young. And your mom's still a looker. I can tell where y'all get it—" I pause when she laughs loudly.

My neck blazes like I've stood in the sun for hours. I tend to ramble on when I'm nervous.

"Thanks, Bradley." She blushes.

I nod. "I'm gonna go put this in the grass now."

She nods back and smiles.

I turn and hurry toward the door like I'm on a mission. All the while, I'm thankful nobody else was in the lobby to witness such a monstrosity.

Once I'm outside hammering in the sign, my nerves quit tingling. Every time I pound the stake, I gain back a shred of confidence. Plenty enough to drive across the road and ask the manager of the Pig if I can park my big sign in the corner of their lot. As suspected, he happily agrees.

We've been pretty tight ever since I locked up Rufus for crashing his lawnmower into the grocery store. He's now in rehab, making our town safe from drunken lawnmower driving. As an added bonus, the Pig got a nice new patch of siding and a brand-new paint job out of it.

I back up the small trailer attached to my truck to the edge of the parking lot facing the bank and place the sign.

Perfect. My life-sized photo smiles back at me like a mirror.

"Hey, big dog. You're one good-looking son of a gun."

I tip my hat and hop in my truck, happy to leave this sign as a reminder for all of Apple Cart County that Bradley Manning is here to serve and protect for another four years.

Ashley

The sun dips behind the trees as I pull into Samuel's driveway. He rents the largest house in his neighborhood, even though it's just him and a six-pound bunny.

I grab the stack of papers from my passenger seat and climb out. Samuel doesn't always come in on Saturdays since we close at lunch. I promised him I'd bring by copies of any new loans or large business deals made today when I met him for a walk.

Today is one of those rare fair-weather days when you can go outside without either sweating or shivering. We don't get many of those in Alabama, so it's best to take advantage. Also, Samuel isn't too fond of my preferred method of exercise—goat yoga.

I walk up his porch steps with my ponytail swaying in the slight breeze. Several lawnmowers echo behind me. It's not uncommon to find people around here cutting grass at the same time. Everyone tends to plan their lawn care around Alabama football games.

Samuel is just as bad. He refuses to work on Saturdays when they have an early kickoff.

I went to a game with him once, but didn't care for his friends. Since then, I've made it a point to be busy or sound indifferent if he mentions me going again. There's no nice way to tell someone you don't want to enjoy a football game in a cushy skybox because his friends are all entitled old-money tools.

A few hours around them, and Samuel joins the pack.

I ring the doorbell and shake that thought from my head. Most of the time, he's super sweet to me. Okay, maybe not super sweet, but sweet. And maybe not most of the time, but at least a lot.

The door swings open to Samuel wearing a dry-fit polo shirt and shorts. He's holding Rambo.

"Ashley." He smiles and strokes the bunny's ears.

"Is Rambo wearing a leash?"

"Yeah." He sets the rabbit by our feet. Rambo rubs his chin against my On Clouds. I tilt my foot uncomfortably. He's constantly doing that on everything.

"You ready?" Samuel asks, inching out the door.

"Yeah, but don't you want to put these inside?" I fan the stack of papers.

"Ah, yes." He grabs them and shoves the leash toward me. "Hold this a minute."

I pinch the end of the red rope and stare down at the curious creature rubbing my ankle. I jerk the leash. "Stop that," I whisper-yell.

Rambo turns his neck in a whiplash fashion and wiggles his nose. We stare each other down until Samuel returns and takes the leash.

I brush my fingers over his hand to try and ignite some sort of spark. The kind I felt from the time I started at the bank until . . .

Well, until I really got to know him.

Samuel is handsome, rich, and powerful. Everything I thought I wanted. What he's not is considerate and friendly. His personality is also very vanilla.

If he were in an ice cream sundae, that's what he'd be. Essential to the dish due to his pedigree and place in society, but giving no flavor or reason to overindulge.

We descend the steps slowly for Rambo to hop down at a leisurely pace. I hope he hops faster on flat pavement, or my heart rate may never get up.

The most cardiac exercise I've had today was seeing Bradley. I lick my lips and think back to this morning. When our hands touched, I felt a spark.

Too bad I can't act on that.

He's several years older, the county sheriff, and probably not interested in me like that. Although he did call me "prettiest." Not much of a compliment compared to my parents and nineteen-year-old sister, but still, it made my day.

"Everything run smoothly today?"

Samuel's voice catches me off guard. "Uh, yeah."

I smile thinking about Bradley holding up his political sign. Then I smile wider when I recall his huge sign across the street. That should give me something pleasant to look at when we're slow at work.

Samuel interrupts my train of thought with details about the last Bama game. He brags about how his dad's friend, who's an economics professor, said he's impressed at the amount of business our small-town branch brings in.

I nod now and again to feign interest. In reality, I'm way more impressed by Rambo hopping along at a decent speed.

Samuel stops talking and walking. I walk a few more feet before noticing. His face is scrunched when I look back. It's hard to tell if he's mad or confused. Maybe a little of both.

I follow his gaze to one of Bradley's signs on a neighbor's

lawn.

"What is that doing in my neighborhood?"

My neighborhood sounds a little presumptuous for someone who rents a house in a neighborhood older than both of us put together. But whatever.

"It's a reelection sign. I've seen plenty around."

"But that's a private residence. Those are typically in publicly owned places."

I shrug. "Maybe they're supporters?"

Samuel makes an annoying throaty sound that could pass for a seagull swallowing a floppy fish. I choose to ignore it.

"Maybe we should turn around. I've never seen Rambo walk this far," I suggest.

Samuel snarls his nose at Bradley's sign, then turns on his heels. Rambo's leash jerks when he tries to continue hopping. I turn the same direction as Samuel and walk toward the lowering sunlight.

I try and lighten the mood by explaining how a random old guy in overalls came in the bank this morning to buy a lottery ticket. He was shocked to find out that banks don't sell them, and even more shocked to discover nowhere in our state sells them.

"I wish someone would run against that fool."

"Like run him out of town?"

"That would be even better." A mischievous smile crosses Samuel's face.

"He said he was on his way to Talladega. I doubt he'll be back since we don't have lottery tickets." I laugh.

Samuel shakes his head. "Not that guy. Bradley."

I guess I'm not the only one with Bradley on the brain.

"Why do you care so much about the sheriff election?"

His face sours like he's sucked on a pickle covered in lemon juice. "I don't like him."

I narrow my eyes. He slows down and looks back at me

as we turn toward his house. "What? You like him?"

My cheeks flush. I swallow and conjure up an answer to satisfy my boss/sometimes mild love interest. The last thing I need is to get Samuel on my bad side, but I also don't want to lie.

"He's actually really nice if you'd take the time to get to know him."

Samuel scoffs. "I haven't been able to make it past his arrogance."

I raise a brow. Samuel calling someone else arrogant?

His face breaks free from the scowl, then he turns toward the door as we climb the porch steps. Without looking at me, he unlocks the door and steps inside.

"I'm going to shower. Hang around if you want."

Rambo hops over the threshold and collapses on the floor, all four feet spread like a tiny bearskin rug. I unhook his leash, but he doesn't move. His tiny heart is beating ninety miles an hour. I hurry to the kitchen for some water.

"Here, sweetie." Rambo scoots toward the bowl and laps the water like he's trudged across the desert for days. I guess that's pretty accurate for a tiny animal hopping the pavement in early fall humidity.

I sit beside him and rub his smooth back. "Your daddy shouldn't have made you walk so fast or far." He blinks at me and hiccups, then dips his tiny head again. "If you were mine, I'd let you lie around and eat carrot cake," I whisper closer to his ear.

He rubs his wet chin on my arm. I draw back and wipe my arm against my yoga pants. A toilet flushes in the back of the house. That's my cue to leave.

I stand and blow Rambo a kiss. The last thing I want to do on a Saturday evening is "hang around" and hear Samuel complain about everything and everyone—especially Bradley.

CHAPTER TWO

Ashley

"And I found this one at Paul's store. It's worth at least two hundred dollars on eBay. I just need to mend the dress and reattach her head."

I lift my chin and fight the urge to wince at the creepy porcelain doll on Glenda's desk. She strokes the hair on its hanging head and returns it to a shopping bag.

Most older women knit, sew, or bake with their grandkids or volunteer for things at church and school. Not Glenda. She restores porcelain dolls.

My spirits lift at the sound of footsteps in the lobby. Finally, someone to rescue me from this freak show. Any more dolls, and I'm bound to have nightmares of *Toy Story 4*.

My mood falls quicker than it lifted when Samuel stomps toward us, a sign in hand. Glenda puts the bag under her desk. I sit straighter in my chair.

With our full attention, Samuel lifts Bradley's sign high,

then chucks it in the small trash can by the teller station, only a few feet from us. Glenda and I both flinch when it hits the metal can. A few flecks of grass and dirt fall from the end of the stake where he pulled it from the ground.

Samuel smooths his hand over his hair and turns to Glenda. "Clean that up, please."

She nods, mouth open with shock. I focus on my computer while she hurries for a broom.

Instead of taking my hint to go away, Samuel sits on the edge of my desk. His knobby knee pokes my hand. I move my hand to my lap, away from the keyboard. I open my mouth to ask what he needs, but he beats me to it.

"Who put that sign in front of the bank?"

I glance at the sign, prominently displaying Bradley's name. "It appears Bradley Manning."

Samuel frowns. "Please don't be fresh with me."

Oh, I don't plan on it—in any sense of the word.

"We don't need that on our lawn. This is a financial institution. We have a strict no-soliciting policy." He stands, adjusting his belt.

I blink at his monogrammed belt buckle, then turn back to my computer screen. I don't turn my head until I've heard his footsteps disappear down the hallway toward his office. Maybe he will stay in there a while.

Lately he's spent more and more time in his office or the back storage room. Not that I'm complaining.

It's left me in charge up front. I like making decisions about daily business, and the tellers and Glenda seem to like me doing that as well. Of course, poor Glenda has to be at Samuel's beck and call. Good luck finding a new secretary whenever she gets fed up and retires.

For her sake, I hope she makes bank off creepy dolls on eBay.

She sweeps the dirt and grass into a small pile as our head

teller arrives. Bonnie returns my smile, then stares curiously at the sign and grass as she dodges the trash can to get to her station. I should probably empty that in the large one before Bradley sees it.

But it's too late.

Boots clip the tile floor, and I follow them to a uniform and kind brown eyes under a cowboy hat. The closer he comes to my desk, the more I notice the hint of concern in his pupils.

"Bradley, how are you?"

He pouts and puts his hands on his hips. "Ashley, have you seen my—"

His jaw drops as Glenda pours a dustpan full of dirt on top of his mangled sign in the trash.

"Sign." His voice is full of hurt.

"You'll have to ask Samuel about that."

He nods and sighs. "Say, speaking of Samuel." He steps close enough for me to smell his aftershave and lowers his voice. "Have you noticed anything unusual about him?"

I relax into Bradley's manly scent to counteract all the unusualness that makes up Samuel.

"Well, other than the usual unusual . . ." I drum my fingernails on the desk. "He has cut back to bathing his bunny only once a week."

Bradley's face contorts.

"You've met Rambo, right?"

"Oh." Bradley chuckles. "He bathes that joker weekly?"

I laugh.

"I meant, in particular, has he been doing anything out of the norm for him here at the bank?"

"Other than trash your sign, no."

He frowns and pulls the sign from the can—just in time for Samuel to walk into the lobby. Bradley turns, one hand holding his sign and the other on his hip.

"Morning, Mr. Covington. Do you happen to know how my sign ended up in the trash?" Bradley shakes the sign, and it makes a warped whoosh. Samuel crosses his arms and raises his head. Bonnie, Glenda, and I glance between them like we're witnessing a Wild West duel.

"We have a strict no-soliciting policy at Smart Money Credit Union."

Bradley steps within a few feet of Samuel and taps the sign against his hand. "It's a public business, and I'm a public servant."

"Servant?" Samuel cocks his head.

"I serve and protect every day."

Samuel huffs and turns away from him. "Glenda, I need your help."

"Yes, sir." She circles the teller station and follows him down the hallway.

His steps are long and swift, much like on our walk Saturday. Whenever something upsets him, he morphs into a race walker. I watch them go into his office, then refocus my attention on Bradley and the bent sign.

"Sorry about your sign."

He shrugs. "No worries. My big one is across the road anyhow." He twirls the sign in his hand. "Could I possibly talk to you later about what I was trying to ask before?"

"Yeah." I don't really know where he was going with the weirdness and rabbits, but I always enjoy talking with Bradley.

"Great." His lips curve, causing my stomach to flip.

What if asking about Samuel was some sort of icebreaker? What if Bradley really wants to talk to me about . . . me?

Better yet, what if he wants to talk to me about *us*?

Bradley

"Thanks, I appreciate this, big dog."

"Sure thing, Bradley." Earl Ed exchanges the bags for my cash and exits my office.

The aroma of salmon, rice, and whatever else the master chef cooked up fills the room. I take the bags to my desk and start unpacking the meal.

I'd called the bank and got Glenda. She promised to send Ashley over when her lunch break starts at noon. I have a few minutes to decide on my look.

After a few spritzes of woodsy cologne, I check my appearance in the mirror. Hmm . . . hat or no hat? I take it off and comb at my hair with my fingers. Then I put it back on. I take it off once more, and start to put it back on as the door opens.

Ashley rushes in. "Is everything okay?"

It is now.

"Uh, yeah. Are you okay?"

She nods. "Glenda said you needed to see me ASAP."

"She may have made it sound more urgent than I intended."

"Oh." Ashley's worry gives way to a grin. "I like your hair."

"Thanks." I swipe a hand across my forehead.

"I've never seen you not wear a hat. Even at yoga."

I half smile. "Have you eaten lunch?"

"No, I just left the bank."

I step aside and wave a hand toward my desk. Her eyes shift to the two plates, then she smirks at me.

"Have a seat." I pull out a chair in front of my desk.

"Thank you."

I circle the desk and sit across from her.

"Where did you get all this?"

"Earl Ed."

Her mouth parts as she scans the spread in front of us. "I've never seen anything like this at Double-Drive."

"It's more like a catering deal."

"How thoughtful." Her smile widens.

"I figured you deserved something better than a corn dog."

She laughs.

"And if you're like me, you get tired of alternating Big Butts and Mary's."

"I have been known to eat at Mary's several days in a row."

"Haven't we all." I laugh this time, then nod toward the food. "Go ahead."

Ashley picks up her fork and starts eating. I go to the mini fridge and grab two bottles of cold water.

"Now, back to what I mentioned yesterday."

Ashley's eyes widen as she chews.

"About Samuel."

She swallows and slumps her shoulders. I'm not sure if she's relieved or annoyed that I brought him up, but it's necessary.

"The unusualness?"

"Yeah. I received some tips about him processing an unusual amount of loans for your bank." I take a large bite of fish and resist the urge to moan at the delicious taste hitting my tongue. Earl Ed is something else.

Ashley's forehead wrinkles. "But I'm in charge of loans."

"Exactly."

She sets her fork down and crosses her arms. "Wait. Are you accusing me of suspicious activity?"

"No. Exactly the opposite. I thought you might know of loan activity Samuel has processed."

She unfolds her arms and sighs. "There's a lot Samuel keeps hidden from me and everyone else. But if he's processing loans I'm unaware of, it would have to be outside of our banking system."

I chew a bite of some vegetable medley as I think, then take a sip of water. *Outside of the system.* "You're saying he's doing this not through the bank, but maybe personally?"

She lifts then lowers one shoulder. "I mean, he may use the bank's money, but he's not logging it in the system."

"How much are you around him in a typical day?" I fight back a smile, since her answer to this question can also benefit my personal endeavors.

"Now that you mention it, he has been going in the back room a lot more often and coming through the lobby a lot less." She picks at the rice with her fork. When her face lifts, it's saddened. "I thought maybe he was comfortable with me handling things up front, but I guess he could be hiding something."

I reach across the desk and place my hand on hers. Our eyes lock, and a warmth shoots up my spine. "Ashley, you've done nothing wrong, I assure you. It's a good sign that you trust your boss. However, your boss is Samuel."

She snorts. "Don't remind me."

We share a laugh. She stops after a few seconds and stares at our hands. I'm caressing hers with my thumb. I pull it back quickly and clear my throat.

"You're around Samuel more than anyone else I know. Ashley, I could really use your help on this."

Her face softens. "What do you want me to do?"

Let's see. You can give me your number, go to dinner with me, marry me . . .

I've really got to stop this. I take a deep breath to bring myself back to reality. "I need you to watch him closely at the bank." I lift my palms in surrender. "And it's none of my business what you do in your personal life, but if you two still hang out, maybe keep your ears open for anything he might mention that seems unusual for him."

She nods. "I can do that."

"Good." I smile, causing her to blush.

My neck heats up and I want to grab her hand again. Correction: I want to swipe all the food and paperwork off this desk—maybe even the computer—throw her across it, and kiss her senseless.

Though very tempting, that would be irresponsible on so many levels.

Her nose and eyes scrunch, and I realize I've been staring at her with a goofy grin. I shake my head. "Yeah, so, if you could keep your eyes and ears open to anything out of the ordinary or anything that might point to some extra loans funneling through the credit union . . ."

She nods. "Got it." Her eyes scan the ceiling and her lips twist.

I concentrate on the fullness of her pink mouth and fall back into my kissing fantasy. Luckily, she speaks, and I rejoin reality.

"And what happens if I notice anything? Like do I call you, or will you check in?"

"I'd already planned on popping in now and again to try and catch him doing something routinely weird. Other than washing rabbits." I wink.

She giggles, sending more heat up my spine. Ashley's laughter could save me a lot of trips to the chiropractor.

She eats another bite, then stares at me. "And what happens if he *is* processing extra loans?"

I open my hands. "Depends."

"On what?"

"If they're illegal. Is he doing them in secret to launder money or falsify information, or . . ." I let my voice trail off when I see the doubt set in her eyes.

"Does he not trust me with the important stuff."

"That's not what I meant."

She frowns. "I know you didn't, but that would be true of Samuel."

I finish my water, then clear my throat. "If you don't mind me asking, why do you continue to work for him?"

"I choose to focus on the fact that I'm working for the bank. I like what I do, and I keep moving up in the business. Samuel being the branch manager is like a bad side effect."

"I'd say." I chuckle.

"He has some good qualities, he's just not the easiest to work for."

I press my lips together. My stomach tightens in warning, but I ignore it and say my piece. "It's none of my business, but I never really understood what you see in the guy." I lift a hand. "No offense if you two are still . . ." I slap both my hands together.

Ashley's lips quirk up on one side.

"Are you two together?" I interlock my fingers, as if needing to illustrate my already invasive question.

"Well, we're not that tight." She smiles and pulls my hands apart, then places my palms so there is a sliver of space between them. "More like this, if anything." She stresses the last word, giving me hope.

I stare at her hands holding mine and wonder if there's anything else stupid I can do to prolong her touching me.

Before I can come up with something, she slides her hands away, leaving me posed like a praying mantis.

"To be honest, I don't know what we are. I still hang out with him some after work, but more because I've known him longer than anyone else in Apple Cart. There are times when I think he likes me as more, but he can be very condescending." She sighs. "Like he is to everyone, I suppose."

"You deserve better."

Her eyes light up as they find mine. I didn't mean for that to leave my mouth, but now I'm glad it did.

"I'm serious. You deserve better than condescending and corn dogs. You deserve salmon and respect."

Ashley's eyes widen until she looks like a cartoon princess. I want so badly to kiss her, but I can't. We're in my office, at city hall, and I just asked her to be my informant on what could possibly be the biggest criminal case I've ever cracked.

Before I do something stupid, I stand and put on my hat. "I've kept you long enough. I'm sure you need to get back to work."

"I do." She stands and follows me to the door.

"I'll walk you out."

"Great, I have something for you in my car."

We walk to her tiny black car, and I step back when she opens the door. Her skirt calls my attention when she bends to reach behind the front seat. She pulls out my sign, which is even more beat up than the day before.

"I found this in our big trash can in the break room."

I take it from her and frown. "Thanks."

Ashley wipes her hands together after holding the dirty sign. "I probably wouldn't put a new one at the bank. He'll just destroy it."

I nod. "Guess I'll have to settle for the life-sized version across the street."

She smiles. "My favorite one."

I open my mouth to comment, but she slides into her car and closes the door. I stand with my jaw dropped, watching her drive away.

At least I now have a non-creepy reason for seeing her often.

CHAPTER THREE

Ashley

I drive away from the sheriff's office in a daze. In less than half an hour, I went from thinking something was terribly wrong to thinking Bradley had asked me on a lunch date to thinking Samuel may be doing something illegal.

The latter of those is the most surprising.

Samuel, illegal? This is the man who admitted waiting until his twenty-first birthday to try a sip of wine. The man who always takes his grocery cart back and never cuts grass on Sundays. I'd bet he still has the warning tag on his mattress.

Then again . . . he is a very private person, and awkward at times. Maybe Bradley is on to something. He doesn't seem like the type to make up a possible fraud case. He has enough to keep him busy around here with random meth labs and lawnmower driving accidents.

I pull into a parking space and sigh. When I get out, two

small holes surrounded by grass and dirt catch my eye. If Bradley tries to stake any more signs, our lawn will resemble a minefield.

For his sake and mine, I hope he has a valid reason for checking up on Samuel. It's evident the two don't care for one another. Bradley always stands a little taller and smiles sarcastically when Samuel comes in the room. And Samuel flat-out said he doesn't like Bradley.

Bradley's various smiles cycle through the back of my brain. Is it bad that I memorized his smiles and what they mean? At least what I think they mean.

I'd like to think he reserves a special smile for me.

"Excuse me." Wendall opens the door from the inside and exits the bank. He turns and holds it open for me.

"Thanks." I cross the lobby, happy to see the lunchtime rush has ended.

I empathize with the tellers working the drive-through window this time of day. That was me not all that long ago.

I set my purse under my desk but don't sit down. Curiosity gets the best of me, and I continue toward the hallway leading to all the closed rooms. Samuel's been spending more and more time back here.

Between his office being in the back and our so-called dating life fizzling out over the summer, I'd thought nothing unusual about it. That is, until Bradley planted the possibility of something else in my mind.

Samuel's door is cracked. I glance over my shoulder to make sure nobody is around before peeking inside. I don't see or hear any sign of someone there, so I ease open the door.

I tiptoe toward his desk and crane my neck to see around all the golf decorations. There are no papers on his desk or behind all the decor. I ease around his cushy chair and pull open the top desk drawer.

Teeth whitening strips and paperclips. That's all.

The side drawer has a box of golf balls with the bank logo, a bag of pens with the bank logo, and the latest issue of *Gun & Garden*.

Clearly, I'm not going to find any evidence in here short of hacking his email. I have neither the time nor intelligence to pull that off.

I close the drawer and slide away from the desk. I'm halfway across the room when the door creaks. I leap toward the edge of the room and sandwich myself between the wall and a large bookcase.

The light from the hallway seeps in and I hear someone. Most likely it's Samuel, but I can't risk moving to check. If I can't see him, there's a much better chance he can't see me.

Low whistling confirms my suspicions. I shift slightly so I can see the desk from the corner of my eye.

Samuel rounds it and plops down in his chair. He cracks his knuckles and clicks something on the computer, then mumbles to himself about stocks and stares at the screen.

I try and focus on what he says, but his voice is too low. After a few moments of silence, he sneezes.

"Bless you," I whisper, then slap my hands over my mouth. *Darn my Southern belle upbringing.*

He stands and walks toward the door as I shrink as close to the corner as possible. I need a distraction to get him out of the office. I can't text him, because my phone is in my purse at my desk.

I curl my legs into my chest and sigh. The door shuts and Samuel returns to his chair. He checks his appearance in his phone, then starts snapping selfies. Like a ton of them.

I'm glued to the corner behind the bookcase, trying to figure out what the heck he's doing on the computer. All while pressing my lips tightly in case he sneezes again.

He clicks around on the computer, mumbling to himself. Then he picks his nose and flicks a booger on the floor.

My gag reflex kicks in and my cheeks almost explode as I fight back choking. Only by the grace of God do I manage to stay silent.

He does something else on his phone before looking back at the computer. His face softens from the concentrated stare he's worn since taking the selfies. He's now grinning almost as widely as he did during his personal photoshoot.

"Perfect profile update." He slaps his hands together and laughs. "Christian Mingle, work your magic!"

My eyes almost pop out of my head. I can't decide if I'm relieved or upset that he's going online for a date. On the one hand, he'll probably quit asking me when he needs a date for appearances. Then again, was he already on there while we were attempting to be a couple? He did say *update*.

I roll my eyes. I'd like to update myself. As in date up from Samuel.

I endure a few more minutes of his whistling before I hear Glenda's voice by the door. "Samuel, the Pepsi machine guy is here. He needs you to sign the order."

"Can't Ashley do that? She's on the management list."

I twist my lips. At least he trusts me to pick what drinks we have in the break room.

"She's not at her desk right now."

A shiver travels down my limbs. *What if he asks her to find me?*

"Be right there."

I let go of the breath I didn't realize I was holding and lean my head against the bookcase.

Samuel clicks some things on his computer, then stands and walks out. I wait until I hear the door close before jumping to my feet. My steps are similar to Bambi's dying mother as I try and hurry in heels after my feet have fallen asleep.

I somehow make it to the door and squeeze out like

biscuits busting through a can. I close it and tiptoe toward my desk.

Samuel turns his head toward me when I sit in my chair. He signs the clipboard and hands it back to the Pepsi man.

"Did you just get in from lunch?"

I shake my head. "Bathroom."

He wrinkles his forehead.

"Female stuff."

His face reddens and he walks away. I exhale loudly and turn on my computer. Glenda comes by and nods toward Samuel walking to the back room. "He's probably not going to get enough diet drinks. I like it better when you approve the orders."

I smile. "Thanks."

She smiles back and starts to walk toward the teller window.

"Hey, Glenda?"

She stops and turns. "Yeah?"

I tilt my head for her to come closer, then glance toward the hallway. Samuel isn't within earshot. Unless, of course, he's hiding like I did. When Glenda is close, I ask in a low voice, "Have you noticed anything strange about Samuel lately?"

She pouts and narrows her eyes, as if thinking. After a few seconds, she shakes her head. "Nothing stranger than usual for a guy with a fake tan and a pet rabbit."

I nod. "Good point."

Glenda smiles and continues on her path to the window. I widen my eyes and open the loan statements needing review.

If he is up to something besides nose picking and online dating, he's doing a mighty fine job of hiding it.

Bradley

The oven dings and I pull out my casserole. I'm no Earl Ed, but I can cook. When you live alone on the outskirts of a town with few restaurant choices, you learn out of necessity. It also gives me something to do when all my friends are coupled up.

Even Kyle, my closest friend since high school, has taken up with the goat girl down the road. I'm happy for them and hope they get married one day. But bachelor life is more fun among friends. Sure, I could get out of the house and make new friends. But I'm beyond the age of going out and painting the town.

Though I might not admit this to anyone, I'm ready to settle down.

I stare at the pan. The cornflakes topping my chicken aren't as crispy as I'd like, so I shove it back in the oven on broil.

Ever since I tried some of Earl Ed's cheese potatoes with cornflakes on top, I've been putting cornflakes on everything.

A few minutes on broil does the trick. It's perfect. I turn off the oven and scoop some on a plate to cool. I'll get about three meals from this big pan. One side perk of living the bachelor life.

I could invite Ashley to eat sometime. Girls seem impressed by guys who can do more than grill.

Maybe after this investigation is over. I need to buckle down and get Samuel out of here. I always knew something wasn't right about that guy. What I haven't yet figured out is why a guy from old-money wealth would want to steal from a credit union.

That's like an oil tycoon robbing a gas station.

I pour a glass of tea and take my plate to the living room. The best part of eating alone is I can sit where I want and eat with no shirt.

Until recently, I cooked everything with no shirt too. I learned the hard way that it's best to have a shield between me and the stove when frying bacon.

My favorite streaming service spins when I turn on the TV. Crappy internet is another downfall to living in the sticks. However, I'll take slow internet and limited food sources over living in town any day.

A few bites into my chicken and the TV connects. I find a good true-crime story and settle in. I'd never admit this to anyone, but watching these shows is motivation for me to get out there and solve some serious crimes.

I couldn't imagine not being sheriff since I love my county and all the people in it. But I have a mean detective streak I can't seem to shake. That's why I have to bust Samuel before the Feds get to him. I want to be the one to protect my county and its citizens.

This episode is one of those murder mysteries where the guy killed the woman on their honeymoon. These really make my blood boil.

If you need life insurance money that bad, marry a ninety-year-old woman with heart problems. Give her a reason to smile the last leg of her life, then cash in after you take care of her a spell. Don't ruin some young honey's life because of greed.

Somehow my mind drifts to worst-case scenarios, and the worst I can imagine is Ashley married to Samuel. I shudder at the idea of his overly tanned face zeroing in on her lips.

I've never witnessed them kissing before—thank God!—but I know they have.

I never understood what Ashley saw in him. Or *sees* in him. She didn't give me a clear answer on whether they're dating.

All the more reason for me not to ask her out.

By the time I finish eating, the guy on the show is being questioned about his wife allegedly falling into the Grand Canyon. I roll my eyes and turn off the TV. My time is better spent putting away the leftovers and working out.

Now that I have more room than an RV in my parents' yard, I can actually work out at home. It's probably for the best since the gym is too distracting. All I do is speculate who's on steroids and possibly other illegal substances.

I let the casserole dish soak in the sink after dividing the remains in Tupperware dishes. Then I head to the spare bedroom.

One perk to renting Adrianne's old house is that she once had this room set up like a huge closet. There's still a large mirror in the center, perfect for working out.

I do a few arm circles, then cartwheel across the room to loosen up. Nobody knows I do this. Not even my mama.

It started as a joke when my ex-girlfriend was a cheerleader in high school. I wanted to prove I could do one. Then I liked the way it loosened my limbs and started doing it in secret before football games. Ever since I quit the gym, it's become my new pre-workout ritual.

Once I'm across the room, I cartwheel back before taking a few deep breaths. Then I go to the shelves Adrianne had made for shoes. They're where I store my dumbbells.

The autopilot part of my brain is busy counting bicep-curl reps, while the more creative side is concentrating on Samuel. In particular, how I can prove him guilty. If I don't play this right, it might look like I'm out to get him due to his history with Ashley and the fact that I don't like him. In reality, I want to get him out of our community for the sake of everyone. Those other things will just be icing on the cake.

Fifteen, sixteen . . . Maybe I should've sent someone there undercover to not involve Ashley. Seventeen, eighteen . . . I hope he doesn't suspect Ashley is watching him.

I set the weights down and stare into the mirror. Did I let my wanting to be around her put her in danger?

Surely Samuel wouldn't hurt Ashley. I mean, I'm eighty-nine percent sure he's stealing from the bank and lying about his natural hair color, but the dude's no murderer.

A scene from the crime show flashes through my head. I manage to shake that thought, but not the thought of Samuel. My weights will have to wait.

I chuckle at my own clever pun and hurry to the actual closet inside this room.

It was a dressing room when Adrianne showed me the place. That made no sense to me with the entire room used as a closet, but I saw potential for more.

Anything I come up with at home for a case goes in this room. The back wall is a map of our county with pins to draw boundaries and move hotspots. Meth labs get the most attention, followed by illegal gambling. But this time it's the bank.

I stick a red pushpin in the center of Smart Money Credit Union. Ironically, it's also in the center of the county. Most everyone does business there, including me.

I've got to get to the bottom of this before someone I care about gets hurt—Ashley included.

CHAPTER FOUR

Bradley

Daisy's rooster crows, waking me up at an ungodly hour. I blink my eyes and shove a pillow over my face. I've always known roosters were loud, but it wasn't until moving out here that I discovered they could be heard for a country mile.

I roll over on my stomach and bury my head under the covers. I doze off a time or two before giving up and getting up.

Maybe it's irritability from lack of sleep or the dreams I had about Ashley. Either way, I'm in a fierce mood by the time I've had my coffee.

That's my excuse for passing my office and driving straight to the bank.

I stop at the edge of the parking lot and open the trunk of my police car. A rubber mallet stares back at me. Not one I confiscated from a crime scene, but one I plan to use to make my point.

I grab it and the one sign I tossed in the back before leaving my house. Then I go to the very edge of the bank's grass, close as possible to the road. My nerves tick with every swing of the mallet. This is likely to get clipped by a log truck before Samuel gets to it . . . as I prefer.

He wouldn't dare stand this close to traffic to rip up a sign.

I smile down at my work and return the mallet to the trunk. Whistling, I straighten my hat and head inside the bank. Glenda's gray head shines in the sunlight reflecting from the glass doors. She turns and smiles when she hears me.

I stop whistling and nod. "Morning, Glenda."

"Good morning, Bradley." She continues stacking pens and deposit slips on the lobby table.

My stomach clenches when I notice Ashley's purse on the floor by her desk. That means she's here somewhere.

No backing out now.

The moment I decided I'd stop here before work, I planned to do three things. One, put up a new sign. Two, ask Ashley to dinner. Three, try one of the mystery-flavor suckers.

I cross the floor and sit in the chair facing Ashley's desk. A bucket of suckers sits beside her family's photo. I admire her beautiful smile, then rummage through the barrel for the flavor I've never had the courage to try. Mystery flavor. The wrapper sticks out like a sore thumb among all the cotton candy and fruit flavors.

I grab it and undo the wrapper before I chicken out. It's a golden color. I've got my hopes up for some sort of honey or toffee.

Nope. Butterscotch.

My lips pucker and I gag. I jump to my feet and hurry to a nearby trash can. After coughing up what sounds like a lung, I wipe my mouth with the back of my hand and turn around.

Ashley stands at her desk with a stack of papers in hand, staring at me. "Are you okay?"

I nod. "Don't trust the mystery-flavored suckers."

She laughs, then pulls a tissue from her desk drawer. "Here."

"Thanks." I take it slowly so I can touch her hand in the process.

Her fingernails are a pretty shade today. I'm not sure what the actual color is called, so I'll call it Ashley. A few seconds pass before I realize I'm still staring at her.

I look away and blot my mouth, then sit back in a chair and toss the wadded tissue into the trash can.

She sits at her desk and adjusts the papers neatly in the corner.

I bet her house is neat too. I start to imagine being in Ashley's house, then remember she still lives with her parents. That doesn't have the same allure, no matter if it's neat.

My neck itches at the reminder of our age gap. Not a lot of years, but I have been on my own for some time. Of course, I lived in my parents' yard until a few months ago. But at least not under their roof.

Stick with it. You have one task left to do. The proverbial devil on my shoulder wants me to ask her on a date. The angel on the other side says lunch in my office. I always tend to fall somewhere in between the two. Dinner with work implications attached seems like a safe bet.

If I can taste a nasty sucker, I can ask her to share a meal at my home. Besides, it's on my to-do list.

"Other than the choking, how are you this morning?" Ashley smiles.

"Good." I run my finger under my collar to combat the itchy neck syndrome. "How's it been going here?"

She glances around the lobby. "Same as always."

I wink, and she blushes. It wasn't intended as flirting, but I'm totally on board with her interpreting it that way.

"A few interesting things, but nothing to worry about." She smiles.

"Maybe we could talk more over dinner sometime." Ashley's eyes trail over my head. I spit out the rest before she makes eye contact again and I lose my courage. "Say Friday night at my place?"

Ashley's eyes fall to mine, but her expression is one of panic.

"She has plans Friday night," a familiar voice calls behind me.

I turn to Samuel. He has his arms crossed, and a large gold watch peeks out from under his suit coat like a rapper on an album cover. I frown and look at Ashley.

Her eyes are on Samuel. "I do have plans Friday night?"

"Yes, remember I said I had a surprise for you on Friday?"

She tilts her head. "No, I don't remember."

"That's because it was supposed to be a surprise, so I'm certain I forgot to mention it."

"So I guess it's not a surprise now." I laugh.

Samuel glares through me. "Did you need anything from the bank today?"

I stand. "Not that you can help me with." I size him up, taking pleasure in having a few inches on him. I turn to Ashley. "Talk to you later, Miss Ashley."

"Bye." She gives me a half smile, then sighs.

I leave without looking back. Every nerve in my body is on fire. My fingers shake when I crank the car and drive toward the road.

The new sign catches my eye, and my anger gets the best of me. I park, get out, and punch the sign with my fist. It relieves a bit of tension, so I do it again, then again. My sign is lopsided and warped by the time I step back and adjust my hat.

An older car is behind my cop car, waiting for me to go. I recognize Kyle's grandparents and go to the passenger window. Mrs. Maudy rolls it down cautiously.

"Morning, Mr. Hubert, Mrs. Maudy." I nod. "Hope I can count on y'all for the reelection."

Hubert narrows his eyes like I'm a psychopath and rolls up the window. I sigh, then get in my car and leave.

That could've gone better, but also worse. Good thing I'm running unopposed.

Ashley

I close out the last of my reports for the day while I wait for the tellers to finish counting down their drawers. Numbers blur across the screen, and I blink my tired eyes. The soothing swish of bills being shuffled is overpowered by a slammed door. I flinch and turn my head to Samuel coming from the back.

Chills run down my spine as I imagine him doing something along the lines of printing fake bills or forging his name on foreclosed properties. Who knows what he's up to?

If anything.

I breathe deeply and remind myself that it could be nothing more than boring bank paperwork.

He walks toward me, and I force a smile. Why did I agree to this so-called surprise? He caught me off guard, which is my weakness. I'm not good at saying no in a panic.

"Ready for your surprise?"

"Yeah." I watch my computer shut down and grab my purse. "Am I dressed well enough?"

"Of course." Samuel unbuttons his sleeves and rolls up the cuffs, as if proving we don't need to look top-notch. "Come on." He motions his head toward the door.

"Shouldn't one of us wait and close the bank?"

"Bonnie's got it."

I glance at Bonnie, who's carrying the drawers to the vault. She's used to closing up the teller station and vault, but Samuel or I always lock all the main doors.

He reaches for my arm. "She's got this. Let's go."

I hesitate a split second before allowing him to lead me to his car.

Like most outings with Samuel, the conversation quickly turns to him talking about himself. I zone in and out, only perking up when I notice we're headed in the direction of my house.

I sit up straighter and stare out the window. "Are you taking me home?"

"No. But we are in Moonshine County."

I fight the urge to say I know that and pay attention to the road. When he turns down a dirt road, sweat beads on my brow. We're in a Mercedes that I'm certain has never come close to gravel, much less dirt.

Either Samuel is lost, or he's planning to murder me.

I rest my hand on the door handle and silently pray it's not one of those childproof locks. Just in case things go the wrong way.

My eyes bug when we pull up to Catfish Camp. I've been here several times before, and my parents come here now and again for a Kiwanis meeting.

Nothing about the place would appeal to Samuel.

He parks near the entrance, and the large catfish mounted above the sign stares down at us. I stare at Samuel, waiting on him to say this is all a practical joke.

"When does the surprise come?" I ask after a minute of silence.

He smiles. "This is it."

The hook in the fish's mouth sways in the slight breeze. I like catfish as much as the next Alabamian, but something smells fishy about Samuel coming here. I wrinkle my nose at him.

"A customer told me they have the best seafood around."

Considering they're the only place within fifty miles to get shrimp that's not fried, I'll give him that. I shrug and follow him to the door.

The screen door squeaks when he opens it. I go in first, and he places his hand on the small of my back. Does that mean he views this as a date? You never know with Samuel.

He looks a little lost, so I step toward the counter. That not only gets the hostess's attention, but also moves me out of reach from Samuel.

"How many?"

"Two."

She smiles at me and grabs two rolls of silverware out of a tin bucket. Samuel eyes the catfish mounted across the walls as we follow her to a small table in the corner with mismatched chairs.

"My name is Marsha. What can I get you two to drink?"

"Water is fine," I answer.

Samuel stares at the empty table before looking at her. "Sweet tea with lemon, and could we please get menus?"

Marsha laughs. "We don't have menus."

"Really?" He scoffs.

"This is a buffet. All you can eat." She fans a hand toward the long buffet tables.

Samuel lifts his chin, and his eyes narrow on the people crowded around them. I'm not sure he's ever been to a buffet aside from fancy weddings and catered skybox events.

"You can fix your supper when you're ready. Plates are on the end." She smiles, then hurries toward the back of the restaurant.

"I didn't know this was a buffet." Samuel stares at me with his mouth parted.

"Surprise." I try not to sound too sarcastic, but don't fully succeed.

He sighs and follows me to the buffet. We both take a plate, and I start down the line. It takes him a minute to join me. I guess he's still in denial.

"Where is all the lobster and sushi?"

I laugh. "Did you really expect somewhere with a catfish on the building to have lobster and sushi?"

He shrugs. "That's my idea of seafood."

"Here is most people's idea of seafood." I grab some boiled shrimp with tongs and plop them on his plate. "Fresh from the Gulf Coast."

I leave Samuel to stare at his plate and survey the other options. Another hand touches mine when I reach for the tongs to the hush puppies.

"Hey, Ashley." Adrianne's face lights up in the glow of the heat lamp above us.

"Hey. Funny seeing you here."

"Same." She laughs. "JoJo and I bring Grandpa Joe here a lot."

I nod.

"What brings you here?"

"I'm actually here with Samuel."

"Interesting." Adrianne's eyes widen.

I bite my bottom lip and nod. "It is."

"Hey, do you know if they have anything gluten free?" Samuel's voice makes me flinch.

I turn to him behind me. "Uh, I'm going to say no."

"They have coleslaw and green beans," Adrianne offers.

He frowns and heads toward the side dishes. I sigh. Adrianne snarls at him, then gives me a sympathetic face. "Good to see you, Ashley."

"You too. Tell Grandpa Joe hi for me."

"I will."

Samuel beats me back to our table. Marsha brings our drinks and a fresh roll of paper towels for the table. I thank her.

"You're welcome. Flag me down if you need a refill."

Samuel frowns and tucks his tie in the neck of his shirt, then grabs a paper towel and stuffs it in the neck as well. I unroll my fork and try to ignore his weirdness. How I ever found this man attractive is beyond my current comprehension.

For the first time, I notice all his quirks. How he doesn't want any of his food to touch and is obsessed with keeping his shirt spotless. It's like his attractiveness overshadowed all his weirdness—until now.

If that's not enough, he spins everything to make himself look better. Like the conversation I'm trapped in now.

"And then I told him I'm sure I could've played football if I'd wanted, but it's such a barbaric sport." He laughs.

I nod between bites of food as if I'm listening. Samuel is so self-absorbed and boring that I want to stab him with my catfish skeleton.

But that is totally inappropriate. What's not inappropriate is bringing up "us." I wait until he takes a breather to eat a bite, then speak. "Samuel, where do you see us going?"

He laughs. "Going?"

"Yeah, from here?"

"Back to the bank to get your car."

I huff and pop a hush puppy in my mouth. That answered my question. He has no interest in being with me. He just wants to keep me from being with Bradley.

Some surprise.

I wave bye to Adrianne from across the restaurant when Samuel and I pay for our food. He examines the receipt on the way to his car.

"That seems like a lot for what we ate."

"It's an all-you-can-eat buffet. Most people get their money's worth."

He shakes his head. "I'll know better next time."

"Next time?" I can't imagine him coming back to Catfish Camp.

"Yeah, next time someone from the bank recommends a restaurant."

Okay, that "next time" makes sense.

The only light for the parking lot is the restaurant lights shining through the windows and one large bug zapper. It's the blue fluorescent kind that sounds like a power line going down when a bug flies inside.

It glistens, giving off enough light for us to find our footing to the Mercedes. Not that we would have trouble locating it among all the mud trucks and minivans.

I climb in the passenger side and yawn. The weirdness of this night alone has been exhausting.

Either Samuel is tired as well or he has some empathy for me, because he doesn't make mindless small talk. We ride in silence until we're close to the county line. Suddenly the car shakes, jolting me to attention.

Samuel slows down and eventually pulls over. I sit patiently while he gets out and walks around the car. He curses loudly and circles again. I get out just in time for him to kick his wheel and hurt his foot.

"What in the world?"

He points to a tire. "My hubcaps are missing!"

"Well, you did park a Mercedes in the dark in Moonshine County."

He bends at the waist and yells.

"So, like, can we drive it?" I wince.

He lifts his head and groans.

Of all the people to be stranded with . . . I shake my head and return to the car. From the comfort of my seat, I watch him through the windshield. He frantically talks to someone on his phone.

I blink my eyes shut and doze off for a few minutes. Then a blue light flashes in my face. A state trooper gets out and talks to Samuel.

By the animated movements of Samuel's hands, I can tell he's describing what happened. I get out if for no other reason than to have a cop know I'm here. Just in case Samuel can't manage to drive home.

The trooper opens the trunk and finds a tool I'm sure Samuel didn't know existed. He tightens our tire and makes Samuel promise to get replacement hubcaps. In turn, he promises to find out who stole the originals.

Samuel's face brightens immediately. "I'm so glad to have met you." He pulls out his wallet.

The trooper stands and shakes his hand toward him. "No, I can't accept payment."

"No, I want to give you my card." Samuel hands him a business card. "In case you ever need a favor in return."

He steps closer to the front of the car, and I read "Hopper" on his badge. He pockets the card and shakes Samuel's hand. "Nice to meet you, sir." Hopper nods at me. "Ma'am."

"Thank you."

He half smiles. "You two drive safely."

I return to my seat and watch Hopper turn off his blue lights. He waits until we go, then drives behind us for a few miles.

We cross the county line and head for the bank. Samuel sings Hopper's praises and comments that he lives in Apple Cart County.

I've never met the man, but my main interaction with anyone in Apple Cart is through the bank. If he doesn't bank with us or go to goat yoga, then it makes sense for me to not know him.

When the bank sign comes into view, I perk up like a dog who's spotted its favorite pee spot. I'm that much closer to my own car.

I'm already opening the door when Samuel parks. He furrows his brow at me, and I decide to use some manners. "Thanks for dinner."

Instead of the expected "you're welcome," he reaches for my face and pulls me toward him. Our lips are inching closer when my stomach cramps.

I do NOT want to kiss him. Not tonight, and maybe not ever again.

I dip my head, causing him to kiss my hair. He slowly slides back, and I escape the hubcap-handicapped Mercedes.

Samuel drives away before I have a chance to crank my Toyota. I don't blame him. What I do blame him for is wasting my time tonight.

I could've spent the evening doing anything else—with *anyone* else.

Samuel may or may not be a criminal, but he is selfish.

And if Bradley thinks he's up to no good, then that's all I need to keep an eye open for more weirdness.

Next time, he can find someone online to go eat catfish with him. And I hope they catfish him!

CHAPTER FIVE

Bradley

I wipe my feet on Jack's doormat and try to knock on the door without disturbing the large wreath.

None of this existed before he married Bianca. What did exist was consistent poker nights.

Jack, Tanner, then Jonah. Even JoJo is married now. We all suspect Kyle is next. Right now, he's in that honeymoon dating phase where he doesn't want to waste a minute he isn't working without Daisy.

"Come in," someone yells from the other side.

I open the door to Jack's two labs wagging their tails. "Hey, ladies." I pet both on the head before weaving between them.

"Kyle didn't come with you?" Jack asks without looking up.

"Nope. He's with Daisy."

Everyone nods or groans.

"Give them a bit, and they'll be ready to join the guys' and girls' nights," Tanner says.

"Is that where all your women are?" I pull out a chair and sit beside Jonah.

"Yeah, shopping," Jonah tells me.

Jack shuffles the cards and sets them on the table. Tanner cuts the stack as Jack gets up. "Bradley, what can I get you to drink?" he calls from the refrigerator.

"Tea is fine."

"Anyone else?"

"I'll take more tea too, cuz." Tanner smiles.

"Cuz?" Jonah and I say in unison.

"Isn't that my term of endearment for him?" Jonah asks.

Tanner laughs. "I guess I haven't told y'all yet."

"Uh-oh." Jack brings back two teas in red Solo cups and sets them beside us.

"Thanks," I say.

He nods and takes his seat.

"So Taylor had to do this family tree thing for school." Tanner's face lights up at the mention of his stepdaughter.

I'm far from wanting kids myself, but I do get a little jealous of the smile he's wearing. I'd give about anything to care about someone that much. The enthusiasm he gets when he talks about Taylor or her mom, Hannah, makes me think he's gotten into something illegal.

Thinking of illegal brings me back to Samuel. Ugh. I can't go one day without that weirdo ruining my thoughts. It's bad enough that he's all chummy with the girl I like. I chug my tea and refocus on Tanner's story.

"And that's how we found out Jack and me are ninth cousins, twice removed."

Jack smiles. "How cool is that?"

"No wonder you guys have always been so close," I say.

Everyone is amused by this news except for Jonah. He stares blankly at Tanner with his jaw dropped.

"You okay, Jonah?" Jack asks.

Jonah blinks.

"What's wrong, cuz?" Tanner slaps Jonah's arm and gives it a shake.

Jonah's eyes widen, and he takes a deep breath before responding. "Dude, I'm married to your sister!"

"Yeah, but it's not like y'all have kids together," Tanner says. He casually sips his tea and starts dealing cards. Clearly, the whole married-cousins thing hasn't sunk in yet.

"But we will one day," Jonah says. His words are clipped and matter-of-fact.

Jack raises his eyebrows at me.

"Why would Taylor do your ancestors anyway? Wouldn't she do her dad's?" I ask.

"Well yeah, but remember me saying I got all interested and then ordered one of those kits for me where you send off your spit?"

I shake my head.

"Bradley, man, where were you? I just said it."

I wipe a hand down my face. "I'm sorry, big dog. I've got a lot on my mind."

"Yeah, you do seem a little spaced out." Jack waves his hand in front of my face. "Maybe I should check the expiration date on that tea." He slides his chair back and returns to the refrigerator.

"I'm fine, guys."

"You don't look fine," Tanner argues.

Samuel's laughing face pops in my mind. *Now I'm not fine.*

I down the rest of my tea and carry the cup to the sink. Samuel haunts the back of my brain like a lost lead on a case.

"I don't know if I can play cards tonight, guys. My brain is fried."

Jonah stares at the cup I tossed in the sink. "I hope it's not the tea."

I laugh. "It's not, trust me." I glance back at him staring down Tanner.

"Good luck with your family tonight." I wink at Tanner. "Call me if things get out of hand."

"Will do." He smirks.

I wave to the others on my way out. Jonah never breaks his glare on Tanner, even when Tanner smiles and waves back.

The last thing I need is to lose my shirt in poker tonight. I hop in my truck and creep down the dirt drive leaving Jack's land. I have plenty of time to think on the way toward my house.

That also means time to talk myself into doing something stupid—like detouring into Samuel's neighborhood and parking down the road from his house. I climb out the passenger side of my truck since the driver's door is extra squeaky.

Armed with nothing but my phone, I tiptoe down the road, avoiding the few streetlights until I come to his mailbox. The lights are on in an upstairs room.

Channeling the stealthy skills that helped me tip cows and toilet-paper houses in my younger years, I sneak beside the house and climb a tree. One large branch stretches beside the room with the light. I carefully lie across it and peek through the leaves.

From my position, I can see the TV screen and the back of Samuel's head in a chair. Who under fifty watches ESPN classics?

The answer would be Samuel. I slide a little farther out the limb to peek inside the room. He doesn't move until a commercial. It's one of those where a popular actor from the eighties is advertising investing in gold. More proof that nobody under fifty watches this stuff.

Samuel stands and turns toward the window. He's wearing a puffy robe like some pro boxer or rich playboy.

I ball up on the branch, careful not to rustle any leaves. He narrows his eyes, then turns around. He walks closer to me, and I scrunch back toward the trunk of the tree.

A brighter light comes on beside the window. I raise up enough to see that it's fluorescent. I manage to slide myself to standing and lean against the branch for a better view.

I bite my tongue to keep from laughing. This dude has a tanning bed!

As I'm turning my head to get a better view of the rest of his room, Samuel stops in front of the window and throws off his robe, revealing a scrawny tan rear.

My eyes bug, and I forget I'm in a tree. I lean back and lift my arm to shield my eyes. That throws me off balance, and I tumble downward, grabbing for branches on my way.

I finally hold tight to one a few feet off the ground. When I lower my feet, I'm standing. By the burn on my arms, I pretty sure they're scratched up. A dog howls a few houses over, and I duck behind the tree.

I hurry to my truck and drive home, breaking every speed limit I've set in this county.

Ashley

I slow my car and a wait for a pack of goats to cross.

Is pack the right word? Maybe it's herd or school. Whatever. Daisy would know.

A goat with a bright collar leads the group toward the chicken coop. I've joked with Daisy that she may as well open a petting zoo. As if she doesn't have enough going on with making candles, giving massages, and teaching goat yoga.

I park beside Hannah's car and take a deep breath. This is the first time I've felt somewhat relaxed all day.

After my awkward surprise Friday night with Samuel, I spent the weekend lying low. I had as little interaction with him at work today as possible. Lucky for me, Mondays are busy at the bank, and he spent ninety percent of the day in his office or the back room. Although that also made me suspicious of what he's up to.

In the years I've worked there, he's gone from spending a lot of time up front greeting people and checking on employees to hanging in the back. Christian Mingle can't take up that much of his time—can it?

I shake my head to try and dislodge any accusations of illegal activity.

A chicken pecks at my shoe when I open the door. I jump back and clutch my fist against my chest. Good thing the nights have gotten a little cooler, or I'd be wearing flip-flops instead of tennis shoes.

"You okay?" Bradley's voice comes out of nowhere like a calming presence.

I turn to him walking toward my car. "Hey, I didn't know you were here."

He nods at Daisy's house. "Goat yoga night, right?"

I laugh. "Yeah." I flinch when the chicken makes a noise.

Bradley bends and picks it up. He's wearing joggers and a T-shirt. I've never seen him in anything besides his sheriff uniform or church clothes. Even the few times he's come to yoga, he was in uniform.

My eyes trail his chest, defined against the fitted shirt. I admire his biceps before noticing terrible scratches on his arms. Picking up a crazy chicken might gain him a few more.

"You didn't get those scratches from a chicken, did you?"

He chuckles. "Nah, I fell out of a tree."

My eyes widen. "What were you doing in a tree?"

His face reddens. "Stakeout."

I wrinkle my forehead. Something tells me to not ask for details. I don't like knowing bad things, even about Samuel. But the more I learn about him, it all adds up.

Bradley makes some kind of sweet noises in a baby voice to the chicken before walking to the coop and releasing it.

"Hmm, it seems to like you."

"Looks like it liked you too."

I wince. "Yeah. I'm not a big fan of birds."

"Really?"

"The whole flapping-wings thing is awkward."

He laughs hard. I smile.

"I've never seen you wear a cap."

"I did all the time before becoming sheriff. Since I had the day off, it seemed silly to suit up."

"Suit up?"

"In uniform."

I smirk. "You make it sound like you're a superhero."

"You never know." He winks.

My insides flame.

Aniston rolls up in her van, slinging gravel toward us. Bradley pulls me against him and turns his back to her vehicle. My heart races as he continues to hold me while she barrels out and jogs up the porch steps.

He slowly releases me and takes a step back. We lock eyes for a split second, and I can't help but think that he had a very superhero reaction in protecting me from flying gravel and crazy chickens.

"She's always late, so we best get inside," Bradley comments.

I part my mouth to speak, but my voice won't work. I nod in agreement and follow him inside.

Everyone is on a mat, most of them chatting. Daisy stands in the front, scrolling on her phone. We grab two mats before she finds her music and calls people out for tardiness. She's the most professional person I know who shares a room with a goat. Actually, she's the only person I know who shares a room with a goat.

Bradley and I go to the back. Our fingers brush when he reaches for my mat. He rolls it out beside his, and all eyes are on us. Several smirks let me know what they're thinking. I swallow and force a smile.

I squirm on my mat and focus on Daisy. She's smirking at us too.

Well darn.

I twist my lips and fall into a stretch. The tame-ish, yoga-approved goats come from down the hall, taking some of the focus off us.

Daisy begins the actual class, and I find myself smiling every time I twist to face Bradley. Between his biceps and chiseled jaw, I might just melt. And it has nothing to do with the heat in this crowded room or the goat marching up my spine.

I spend the rest of the night sneaking glances at Bradley, silently comparing him to Samuel. He's stronger and more masculine. He's also more handsome than Samuel without even trying. I always enjoy him in uniform, or "suited up" as he says, but he somehow manages to make sweatpants attractive.

Most of all, he's here, doing yoga beside me, without complaining.

Not that I need a guy to like yoga, but I do need a guy open to doing things I like once in a while. Bradley's so easygoing. I bet I could even convince him to watch the *Barbie* movie with me.

"Umph." A goat jumps off my shoulders, jolting me back to reality.

"Are you okay?" Bradley whispers.

I nod. His face is full of concern. My stomach tingles at his sincere care. Daisy calls out another move, and I turn my face away from him. For once I'm glad, because I'm certain I'm blushing.

I pretend to concentrate on Daisy's instructions, when in reality I follow her in movement only. My mind is swirling a smoothie of thoughts made up of Bradley and Samuel. I purse my lips and snarl. That is not a good mixture.

By the time Daisy bids us namaste, I've made up my mind about Samuel. Even if he's completely innocent, he's not a nice guy. Chances are, he is up to something rotten. Bradley has no reason to make up a suspicion.

"Here." Hannah turns around and hands me some spray to clean my mat.

"Oh thanks." I take it, along with the clean towel I set aside to wipe it down. I watch Bradley from the corner of my eye as I meticulously wipe both sides. He is cleaning his own mat with another bottle and finishes before me.

Figures. Most guys don't spend enough time on cleaning. Except he then rolls up his mat with the speed and precision of a ninja warrior. Maybe he's just that good.

My eyes trail him toward the front, and I clumsily stand with my mat and towels. I set the bottle of spray next to Aniston, who is still propped on her mat, carrying on a conversation with Carolina. Then I hurry after Bradley while rolling my mat.

I stick the sloppy roll in the pile of clean mats and catch up with him in the parking lot. "Bradley."

He turns and shoves his hands in his pockets, causing his arms to flex. I swallow and silently hope he did that on purpose, for me, and not to warm his hands.

"Hey, sorry I didn't say bye. I've got something in the Crock-Pot at home that needs stirring."

My brow twitches. For a millisecond I imagine myself going to Bradley's house for a home-cooked meal. Then I snap back to reality when a goat bleats behind me. I hop forward, hitting Bradley's chest.

He laughs. "It's just Mullet." He pets the goat on the head and makes the same baby talk he did with the chicken.

Okay, yoga, cooking, and sweet talking to animals. He's got to stop this before I propose.

"Anyway." I shake my head and take a tiny step away from him. "I wanted to say that I'm all in."

He lifts his head from Mullet to me and narrows his eyes.

My cheeks flush when I realize how I must sound. "With keeping an eye on Samuel," I clarify before taking a bigger step back.

"Oh."

"If he's up to something sketchy, I want to help you."

"No pressure on that. I know you two went out to dinner and all."

I snort. "Trust me, that was not a date."

Bradley's lips curve into a lopsided grin.

"I'll be happy to keep an eye out at work."

"All right. Sounds like a plan." He grins wider, then turns toward his truck, taking a tiny piece of my heart with him.

I watch him for a few seconds, then escape to my own car—before any nosy bodies come out to interrogate me.

CHAPTER SIX

Ashley

The front door swings open to Samuel. He somewhat nods at a few customers, then hurries to the back. I watch him slide into his office and close the door.

According to my computer screen, it's almost nine. And unless he's only used the back door today, which I highly doubt due to his always making a grand entrance, he's just now getting to work.

The head teller and I have been here close to two hours, and everyone else well over an hour to open at eight. I doubt he had car trouble, since he's already replaced his hubcaps and bragged about getting a new alarm over the weekend.

A young couple stops at my desk, so I focus on them and ignore whatever weirdness Samuel is cooking up behind me. "Hi, how can I help you today?"

They introduce themselves. I recognize the woman's name and think she's a schoolteacher.

"We'd like to get a loan for our first home."

My mouth curves at the happiness and excitement on their faces. One day I'd love to purchase my first home, presumably with my husband.

That's the real reason I've stayed at my parents' house. Not for lack of funds. I've seen a few cute little rentals around Apple Cart, and my hometown as well. But I'd much rather wait and pick out a home to own with my forever partner.

"What do you need from us?"

"Oh sorry." I giggle and hope they didn't notice my daydreaming. "Do you already bank with us?"

"Yes," the man answers.

I go through the routine of looking up their info. I'm halfway through finding out what they can get for a loan when Samuel comes by and sits on the edge of my desk.

Locusts may as well have crawled out of my computer, because that's the instant reaction I have in rolling my chair away. "Can I help you?"

"I need you to make some copies for me."

I smile at the couple before turning to him. "I'm with customers."

Samuel puts on a fake smile for them, then stands and adjusts his monogrammed belt buckle. I shift my eyes away from his torso and scrunch my nose as he slides past me.

"Soon as you finish with them, meet me in the back."

I give him a quick nod, then turn to the normal people in the room.

"Thanks for your business," he says loudly behind me.

I flinch and press my lips together until the sound of his dress shoes connecting with the tile floor fades away. "Where were we?"

I live vicariously through their excitement of joint home ownership for the next half hour. I've almost forgotten about

GUILTY OF LOVE

Samuel until I pull their paperwork from my printer. *Right . . . Samuel's copies.* I puff up my cheeks and stack their papers neatly, taking extra time to avoid my upcoming task for Mr. Grump.

"Here you go. Call me with any questions."

"Thank you," they say in unison.

Both shake my hand before joining their hands and practically skipping out the door. I fold over in my chair and hold my stomach.

"Ashley, are you okay?" I turn my head to Bonnie staring at me from her window.

"Yeah, just stretching." I raise my arms above my head, then stand. "I'll be in the copy room if you need anything."

"Okay." The way she hangs on that word lets me know she doesn't fully believe I'm okay.

I don't fully believe it either. I'm semi-jealous of a nice couple my age buying a home, while paranoid about Samuel's every move. Why can't Glenda make copies? Isn't that why she's here?

Of course Samuel isn't in the copy room. I'm forced to knock on his office door and hope he isn't on some odd virtual mingle date or picking his nose in the corner.

"Come in."

Here we go. I open the door with caution and step inside as if I'm walking into a minefield. At least the lights are on. Sometimes he sits in the dark. I used to find it sultry, but after getting to know him better, I realize it's just sad.

"What copies do you need?"

He stands and smooths his tie, which has a print of hundred-dollar bills. A little petty, if you ask me.

"Come on." I follow him to the back of the copy room. He points to several boxes on the counter near the copier. "I need ten copies of all the papers in these boxes."

"You're kidding."

He puts his hands on his hips. "No, I'm not."

"Where's Glenda?"

"Making coffee."

I frown.

"Look, I'm still your boss. If someone comes in for a loan, I'll handle it or come get you to do it."

I bite my bottom lip to keep from screaming. This has to be punishment for Friday night. Or avoiding him yesterday, or snarling at his belt buckle. Something, anything.

"I've got to go to a meeting. When you're done, put them on my desk, please."

"Okay."

"Thanks." He gives me a smug look.

I sigh and open the first box. Making and sorting ten copies of all this will take me forever. Might as well make myself comfortable.

I kick my heels in the corner and pull my hair back with the hair tie on my wrist. After feeding through about fifty pages and lifting the copier a dozen or so times, I also take off my bracelets. Clearly, I came dressed for working out front and not in here.

About a third of the way through the first box, I prop my arms on the wall and twist to stretch my back. I'm not certain if last night's yoga helped or hurt me.

Muffled voices come from outside. I lean against the wall and recognize one as Samuel's. There's a small window above me. I straighten and listen. The window is too high for me to see whom he's talking to, but it sounds like another man.

"We'll discuss the rest later," Samuel says.

"Ten-four."

I hear footsteps crunching leaves and step away from the window. Glenda stands in the door with a mug of coffee in hand, adjusting her glasses. "You okay, dear?"

"Yes, ma'am." I smooth my hair and laugh nervously.

She peers at my bare feet, and I wiggle my toes. When she meets my gaze again, I push off the wall and fan my face. "This copier has me all hot. I had to lean against this block wall to cool down."

Glenda raises one brow. "Then I guess you wouldn't care for a cup of hot coffee."

"Not at the moment, but thanks." I smile.

When she finally walks away, I return to my penance at the printer. I copy for another hour before I hear a hint of life.

I turn to Samuel clearing his throat. He's propped in the doorway. "Is that the last box?"

I scoff. "More like the bottom of the first."

He frowns.

"How was your meeting?" I attempt to sound kind, but it comes out sarcastic.

"Great, thanks." I can't tell if he's being sincere or better at hiding sarcasm than me.

"I'm going to head to lunch." He steps away from the door frame. Before I can ask if he expects me to stay here while he's gone, he's gone.

I stretch my hands and work through the small stack left in this box. Then I reach for my shoes and bracelets. Someone needs to stay up front for the upcoming lunch hour when we get busy. Someone also needs to find out what Samuel was doing at the edge of the woods with a mystery man.

The security footage. My eyes widen.

It uploads to the cloud, but we keep a backup drive in the vault that overrides itself every night. I can change out the flash drive and see what he was up to today.

Before I rejoin the land of the living in the lobby, I pull my phone from my pocket. I dial Bradley's number.

"Hello?"

"Hey."

"Hey, Ashley."

"I have something to give you tonight."

"Oh?"

"Yeah, can you swing by the bank later?"

"Maybe, I'm on a secret mission right now."

"Oh." My mouth parts. *Is this about Samuel too?*

"Tell you what, swing by the Pig when you get off. I'm patrolling there tonight. They're putting out signs for a meat sale, and things get crazy when that happens."

"Okay."

"See ya then."

I slide my phone back in my pocket and hurry out front. I best grab that footage before rush hour.

Bradley

I stare at my phone. Ashley's sweet voice still echoes in my ear.

What could she possibly have for me? Most likely something to do with Samuel. That's all good, but I allow myself to fantasize it's more personal.

Gravel crackles ahead, and I raise my face to Roy's truck barreling down the dirt road. He wanted me to meet him at the Gamer's Paradise drive to pass on his tradition.

Ten years ago, I was eating fried rattlesnake nuggets before playing football against Apple Cart. Back then, I never would've imagined Roy would one day tap me to carry the torch as the rattlesnake provider for the Wisteria Mud Cats.

Yet here I am.

Roy stops beside my truck and rolls down his window. "Thanks for meeting me. I had to deliver some busts to Jack."

"Busts?"

"Deer mounts."

I raise my chin. Clearly my head was in the wrong place on that one.

"You wanna ride with me so nobody sees you in the secret spot?"

I twist my mouth and contemplate his offer. Roy isn't known for breaking the law. Heck, his wife is on the church praise team and makes the best bundt cakes in three counties.

"Sure. Let me park better." I pull my truck into the ditch to not block Jack's drive. But before I get in with Roy, I shove my pistol in my boot. You never know what kind of trouble might come up on a rattlesnake hunt.

Roy strokes his graying beard and stares at me. His face is serious and a little scary. "Bradley, what you're about to see can't be shared with nobody. Not even my kids know this secret, only Luanne. And I only told her after I fell out of the tree stand one year and needed her help preparing the snake."

I nod. "Got it."

Excitement bubbles inside me like I'm approaching the big drop on a roller coaster. The honor of holding the snake secret mixed with anticipation of what the secret holds is almost too much to bear.

Will we kill them ourselves, or is there some kind of underground snake supplier I've never heard of? And what's in the recipe?

Roy grins and pulls onto the main road. I buckle my seat belt and watch the trees go by, anxious to have my questions answered soon.

We cross into Moonshine County. Good thing I brought my gun.

Roy is quiet except for whistling along to the Kenny Rogers 8-track crackling through his truck's speakers. I'm a little confused when we pass all the good dirt roads and head for downtown Sparrow.

I adjust my boot so I can grab my pistol at a moment's notice. Anyone who sells snakes might be doing something illegal on the side. Or maybe selling snakes is his side gig and he does something illegal to pay the bills.

I'm fully prepared to take down some strung-out deadbeat, but Roy pulls into the Pig. This is strange. Couldn't he have stopped for something at our county's Pig, presumably when I wasn't with him?

He parks near the front and turns off the truck. Then he removes his cap, fans his hand over hair too short to mess up, and readjusts his cap. "We're here."

I glance around the parking lot. Aside from having a package store behind the Pig, it's no different than being in Apple Cart County. "Okay?"

"Come on." Roy hops out and slams his door.

I watch him walk a few feet toward the store before getting out. I guess we're going inside. It's not until we're standing in the deli that I realize what's happening.

We're going to a butcher.

I smile to myself. It all makes sense now. Moonshine County is even more backwoods than our neck of the woods. I bet they slaughter snakes on-site.

Ham, chicken breasts, turkey legs. There are even the dreaded chicken feet. I cringe. Yep. This would be the place to buy snake. I follow Roy to the edge of the display, anxious to see what part of the snake we're going to get. My eyes widen when he picks up a pack of chicken gizzards.

"Chicken gizzards?"

"Shhh." He shushes me loudly. "I said don't tell nobody."

I blink.

Roy holds up the pack and winks, then hands me several until my arms are full. He grabs the rest, and I follow him to the front of the store in a daze.

I haven't been this let down since the eighth grade, when I found out Santa was a sham. That's why I work so hard each holiday to make the foster kids believe.

But finding out the special snake I ate every year of varsity football before facing our rival is nothing more than chicken . . . that's downright disheartening. Now I'm second-guessing whether Luanne's sweet potato casserole really has sweet potatoes. Does she gut a pumpkin instead?

I sigh and set my armload of gizzards on the conveyor belt. Roy greets the young cashier and pays for the meat. I wait while the bag boy assembles three paper sacks, then grab them.

When we're back in the truck, I decide it's time to ask questions. "Hey, Roy, if we're just eating chicken gizzards, why come all the way here?"

Roy cranks the truck. Kenny attempts to belt out "The Gambler," but the 8-track hangs up. He beats the dash with his fist and the tape jumps back on track.

"That's better." He pets the dash like it's a dog.

I raise my brow at the weirdness. Not that this should surprise me, given the rest of our journey.

"As for the chicken, gizzards don't last long when Diesel puts on the meat sales."

I nod. The Apple Cart Pig's manager must really discount those gizzards. By the time I'm called in, usually all that's left is more expensive meats like steaks and bacon.

"And if Morgan's working, she'd grill me on why I'm buying so many gizzards for a family of four."

I nod again. "That, I definitely understand."

Roy pulls to the stop sign before the county line and

turns to me. "Sometimes you gotta get out of the county to find what you're looking for."

I smile. "Good advice."

Roy returns my smile, then stares ahead and crosses into our county. He whistles the rest of the way to Jack's drive.

When I reach for my door handle to leave, he speaks up. "I'll holler at you Friday before I cook these so you can come learn how."

"That would be great." I open the door, then pause and turn to him. "I'm curious to see how you make chicken taste like snake."

"I fry them in snake oil."

I cock my head. "Snake oil?"

"Yeah, there used to be a snake-oil salesman come through for Trade Days. After he died, I found a lifetime supply on eBay. It can all be yours now."

I fight laughing. "I'm one lucky man."

"You sure are, Sheriff Bradley Manning."

As soon as I shut the door, Roy barrels toward town, leaving a line of smoke in his path. I climb in my own truck and drive to our Pig. Ashley should be off work anytime.

I pull into the parking lot with a new respect for chicken gizzards. I'm also rethinking all the other "exotic" meats I've eaten over the years. Alligator, squirrel, that emu Kyle found hurt in the woods and grilled for us.

There's a good chance any of those were actually chicken. Especially the emu. I don't see how it could make it all the way from a farm in Mississippi to the woods in Wisteria.

No wonder everyone says stuff tastes like chicken.

I flinch at a soft knock by my ear. Ashley stands outside my car. I smile and roll down the window.

She sticks her hand down her shirt and tugs at something. My neck flares, and sweat beads behind my ears. I'm not sure what she's up to, but I have the urge to handcuff her.

"Here." She holds a tiny flash drive up to my face. I stare like it's a snake.

"It's got the bank surveillance from the past day and a half. I had to sneak it out in my bra before Glenda saw me with it."

I swallow. I never knew a flash drive could be so sexy.

"Thanks." I hold up my palm and allow her to drop it in my hand.

"He was talking to someone outside the bank today, and I'm not sure about what. I'll keep you updated. Maybe what's on here will help."

"Thanks," I say again, as if that's the only word I know.

"You're welcome." She looks behind her. "I best get home. I'm supposed to go to dinner with my sister tonight."

"Okay." Ah, a new word.

Ashley flashes me a smile worthy of an orthodontist advertisement—the "after" photo. Then she turns toward her car, and I watch her walk away.

I tighten my grip on the flash drive. It still has her scent. I shove it in my shirt pocket and head for home. My heart beats fast with it against my chest. If I react this way to a stupid electronic stick, how would I react if she gave me something really special?

Maybe one day I can find out.

CHAPTER SEVEN

Bradley

I watched the entire bank footage last night and found nothing out of the norm for a daily operation of a local branch. However, I appreciate Ashley's gesture, probably more than I should.

For all Samuel's shortcomings, he is smart. If he's doing someone illegal, he wouldn't do it where the cameras can find him.

That's all the more reason to have suspicions about him doing something out of line behind the building. Hmm . . . Ashley really is my greatest source on this one.

I sigh and swipe my hands down my face. I hate putting her in the middle of all this, but I need someone on the inside. If I reach out to other law enforcement, they will have a team of CSI scraping the place like Bernie Madoff ran the operation.

The last thing our county needs is uproar over an alleged

scandal. Although we have quite the cast of colorful characters around town, I still feel obligated to at least attempt to uphold a Mayberry persona.

I grab my hat and head for the parking lot. It's time to get Ashley on board with my plan so I can see if Samuel's really a bad egg or just an egghead. Chances are he's both.

"Well, color me surprised." My sign flaps when a semi-truck passes it. Samuel hasn't taken it down, but he has mutilated it. Lord only knows if he took a knife or a paper shredder to the thing, but my name is barely legible.

Even worse, there is a larger sign in pristine condition next to mine. The words "Vote Vern" stick out like a sore thumb.

Vern. Where have I heard that name before?

My stomach sours like I've overeaten my ex-girlfriend's nannie's corn chowder. It doesn't much matter who Vern is, because he's running for sheriff—against me!

I take a step back and shake my head. Maybe this is some odd mirage.

Nope. No amount of head shaking will make it go away.

I take a deep breath and march toward the bank. I can't let this Vern character distract me from my bigger purpose of getting to the bottom of this Samuel stuff.

The bank door feels like a hundred-pound barbell in my hand. I pull it back and swallow hard. Ashley sits at her desk, the sunlight catching her blonde hair.

Am I a jerk for asking her to be my mole? What if I put her in danger?

She smiles at me, and I'm under her spell. My feet float toward her desk.

"Hey, did you get anything good?" She raises her eyebrows.

Okay, she brought it up, so maybe it's not such a bad idea. I did give her a choice in the matter. And there's a lot worse people I'd rather work in close proximity with than her. Like everyone on the planet.

"Not a lot, but thanks for that." I pull the flash drive from my front pocket and place it in her hand. A warmth rushes up my arm. Our hands linger for a second, then Samuel's voice comes out of nowhere.

"Bradley."

Ashley jerks her hand back and hides the drive in her fist. The combination of her hand moving from mine and Samuel's sleazy voice saying my name makes the hair stand on my neck.

I cringe a little before turning to him. "Hey, Samuel."

"I hope you don't mind sharing a little real estate with your sign."

"Not at all." I grind my teeth into a forced smile.

"Good." He smirks. "And sorry about whatever happened to yours. It was messed up when I came to work."

Yeah, right.

"That's fine. I have plenty around town."

Samuel nods and focuses on Ashley. "Can you get back on making copies after your customer leaves?"

By the sour way he says "customer," I assume he means me.

"Sure." She presses her lips.

Samuel continues past us and opens the vault. He enters and closes it.

Ashley lets out a deep breath. She watches the vault for a moment before turning and wiggling her finger for me to come closer. I lean in and inhale her sweet scent.

"I think he knows where all the cameras are pointing at all times," she whispers.

Her lips brush my ear, sending shivers down my spine. It takes me a second to recover so that I can answer. "I'll see if there's something we can do to monitor him," I whisper in her ear.

She nods, and her hair tickles my neck. I move back to look in her eyes.

"That sign . . ." She frowns. "It's Vernon Hopper."

"Hopper?" My eyes bug and I laugh. "The young state trooper who eats steroids for breakfast?"

She shrugs. "He's bulky." She motions me closer again. I lean in and hold my breath. "Samuel is endorsing him. I'll tell you more later."

I lean back and try not to fall on my butt. Of all the stupid, slimy ways to try and one-up me. I straighten and sigh. "Call me later."

She smiles sympathetically. "Okay."

I turn and nod at the tellers watching us. Lord knows what they're thinking about me—or us. But I don't really care.

My eyes fix on the front door, and I march toward my patrol car. I've learned two things. One: Samuel is out to get me. Two: Ashley is on my side.

That last one is enough to lift my mood.

Ashley

I'm elbow deep in documents when Samuel waltzes into the copy room.

"Ashley, my bunny isn't feeling so well."

"I'm sorry to hear that." My voice is a little sympathetic.

Despite my disdain for Samuel, I do have compassion for Rambo. The poor rabbit can't help he was adopted by a tool.

I resume my menial task, hoping if I ignore the problem, he will go away.

"The housekeeper called and said he's feeling puny, so I'm going to take the rest of the day off."

I raise one brow. "Okay."

"You're free to stop these copies and manage the front."

"Thanks." This time my voice contains no sympathy.

That's the common sense thing that needs to happen, and I wasn't about to wait on his permission.

I let the last page run through the copier, then turn it off. Samuel leaves, and I let out a long sigh.

While I'm straightening the papers and stacking them to save my place for later, it hits me: He's going home for the rest of the day. I peek out the door and glance both ways. He went in the direction of the lobby to leave. His office is locked, but . . .

I tiptoe down the hall and pull the handle on the backroom door. Sure enough, he didn't shut it completely.

My heart pounds as I start to open it. Then I get an idea. I hurry to the copy room, where I left my cell phone, and call Bradley. He answers on the first ring.

"Coast is clear if you want to come find evidence."

"Give me ten."

He hangs up, and a mischievous excitement bubbles inside of me. Something about searching for evidence with Bradley in a secret room excites me. It's like we're in *Romancing the Stone* or something.

I leave the door cracked and head toward the lobby as if it's a normal Thursday afternoon. No sooner than I can log in to check my email, Bradley comes to my desk.

"I have your paperwork ready. Follow me." I stand and refuse to look any coworkers in the eye. It's not unusual for

Samuel to conduct business in his office. Fingers crossed they think that's what we're doing. What else would we be doing in the back?

My chest warms, then the heat crawls up my face. I'm not going to entertain that thought. Instead, I take comfort in the fact that Bradley will protect me from whatever weirdness lives inside the back room.

I ease the door open and blink. Even though I never lived through the eighties, I can imagine this is what it looked like.

Tons of filing cabinets and metal shelves line the walls. In the center of the room is an old boxy computer with a black-and-green screen. A heavy printer with dotted paper sits next to it.

It's like a scene from *Wall Street*. The original movie with cell phones the size of my forearm.

"Either this is some kind of backup for internet outage, or Samuel is trying to bypass y'all's bank server." Bradley drops his hands from his hips and walks toward the computer.

I join him and stare at the screen. It's filled with names of bank customers. Beside them are loans and the amounts. I take the ancient mouse and scroll to see more. My forehead wrinkles when I see Paul's name in bright green. "Wait, this can't be right." I narrow my eyes for a closer look.

"What?"

I turn to Bradley leaning beside me. My cheeks flush, and I stare back at the screen. "Paul's name is down for three different loans. In the years I've worked here, Paul hasn't had an existing loan or gotten a new one."

"What are you saying?" Bradley's brow furrows.

"The man deposits sacks of pennies every week."

Bradley laughs. "No, why do you think he's in there?" He points to the ancient computer.

"I think Samuel may be making up fake loans." I straighten and sigh. "Why would he do that?"

Bradley puffs up his cheeks, then exhales. "To account for where money is going."

I swallow.

"This is textbook money laundering, just without the extra business. Instead of funneling money through a storefront, he's funneling it through the bank."

"But it's not actually in the bank, right?"

He shrugs. "If it's not in your real system, I'd say he's got a stash of cash someplace."

Bradley picks up a piece of paper from a stack beside the printer. More papers follow it, connected by the dotted sides. "If he keeps records and prints these, he can have something to show at a moment's notice if he needs to put the money into the system."

I bite my bottom lip and imagine Samuel making up and printing fake loans. "But if the money's not in the banking system, why do all this? There's plenty of shady people doing cash deals without a big cover-up."

"Because he's probably doing what I feared he was." Bradley lets the papers fall like an accordion as they restack themselves. "He's not putting money in. He's taking it out."

My body tenses at the realization of what's happening. When I'm able to talk, it comes out in a whisper. "For what?"

"Investments, side scams, personal gain. Who knows?" Bradley shakes his head. "Has he splurged on anything unusual and expensive lately?"

"Just a purebred bunny and golden belt buckle."

Bradley raises a brow. "I bet he credited both of those to Paul."

I glance above his head to the shelf in the back. It's filled with boxes just like the ones Samuel brought me to copy.

"Wait." I cross the room and reach for a box at eye level.

It's wedged between two others and rather heavy. I curl my fingers around the lid and pull hard. It loosens and slams into me, pushing me back. I stumble in my heels and almost fall.

Then something catches me.

Bradley.

I catch my breath and hold the box tightly. He steadies me and we lock eyes. If the box weren't so bulky, our faces would be much closer. And if it weren't so heavy . . .

The box starts to slip. Bradley tightens his grip around my waist with one hand and grabs the box with the other. My sides tingle as he effortlessly returns me to standing and scoops the box on the table.

He opens the lid, while I try and pretend like I'm not melting from our little encounter.

"What's in here?" He picks up a single sheet of paper.

I lick my lips and sigh. "I'm afraid it's what Samuel's had me copying the past few days."

Bradley looks confused.

"He brought some boxes like this into the copy room and asked me to make ten copies of each sheet. The papers look old."

Bradley holds the paper closer. "This one is from 2008." He sniffs the sheet. "Or so it says. It isn't musty smelling or faded."

"Should it be?"

He glances around. "This room is musty, and it's in a box that I don't think anyone has moved for some time."

"What's that mean?"

Bradley thumbs through a few more sheets. "All different, random dates and names." He returns the papers and closes the box.

I shift my weight to the other side, as my legs are starting to regain feeling from the almost fall and his hands on me.

"I think Samuel's been typing up random loans and chucking them in these boxes." He nods toward the shelf.

"But why have me make ten copies?"

"Good question. Maybe he needs to send them someplace as proof or is preparing to act as if he's sending them out to cover his butt."

I cross my arms. "And here I was thinking he was just making me do busywork."

"Not to give you more busywork, but think you could make one extra copy next time?" Bradley smirks.

I nod. "Good idea." I scan the corners of the room. "I don't know if we have a camera in here, but I need to pull the surveillance film from today. I have a suspicion he didn't leave entirely for Rambo."

"Rambo?"

"The rabbit."

"Oh." Bradley frowns, then smiles at me. "He's not taking you out again tomorrow night, is he?"

I laugh sarcastically. "Not if my job depended on it."

"Good. How about bringing that footage over to my place then?" He places the box back on the shelf as if it weighs an ounce.

"What time?" I fight a huge grin and try to sound casual.

"Say around nine. I would cook for you earlier, but I've got to direct traffic after the high school game."

"That's fine."

"Good, it's a date." He tips his hat and slides out the door.

I stand in the glow of the green computer screen, wondering exactly what he means by *date*. Then I snap back to reality and leave the room, door cracked like I found it, before someone catches me.

CHAPTER EIGHT

Bradley

It's been a long day, from snooping out a potential meth lab to frying my inaugural batch of chicken gizzards in snake oil with Roy. Something about the fake snake must work, because Wisteria put a whooping on Apple Cart.

Once the parking lot is empty except for cars belonging to players, coaches, and booster club members, I climb in the patrol car and head for my house. I almost turn off the flashing lights, then change my mind so I can drive faster.

I want to be home in time to take a shower before Ashley shows up.

I stop speeding and turn off the blue lights a few miles from my road. The last thing I need is for Daisy's farm animals to go haywire over sirens.

A few times I've considered asking Adrianne and JoJo if they'd sell me this house instead of renting. Then a voice in the back of my mind warns that I might want to wait until I find who I'm going to marry. She would want to pick out a house, and I imagine the resale value being low for a tiny house in the middle of the woods.

I unlock the door and go straight for the shower. I need time for my hair to set before Ashley gets here.

Yes, set. I have a foolproof method that started in high school. I comb my damp hair, then cover it with a hat. That slicks down any potential cowlicks or flyaways.

Of course, I've never admitted this to anyone. It's more fun to pretend I have perfect hair.

I shower, shave, and implement my hair-styling secret in record time. It takes me longest to decide which T-shirt to wear. I want to look casual and comfortable at home without looking slouchy.

Her car pulls up as I'm microwaving a bag of popcorn. I toss the cap I'm wearing on the counter and take a deep breath when she knocks on the door.

"Hi." Her sweet voice greets me when I open it.

She's wearing jeans that hug her legs and a bright shirt. I try not to stare and motion her inside. "Come in."

She walks in and pulls a flash drive from her jeans pocket. I take it and halfway resent it not coming from where it did before.

Ashley glances around my small living area as I close the door.

"You can have a seat on the couch. I can get you a drink. What do you like?"

"Water is fine." She smiles.

The microwave beeps on my way to the kitchen. I shove the flash drive in my own pocket, then grab the popcorn bag full-fisted without thinking. I drop it on the ground and shake my pulsing hand. Cupping it around a bottle of water gives me a little relief.

I grab a Dr. Pepper for myself and carefully pour the

popcorn in a bowl. When I enter the living room, Ashley's standing across the room, staring at my trophy shelf.

I set the snacks on the coffee table in front of the couch, and she turns her head. "You still have trophies from high school?"

"Yeah, don't you?"

"Maybe in the attic, but not on display in the living room." She laughs.

I palm the back of my neck and turn so she can't see the embarrassment on my face. Nothing says "peaked in high school" quite like having your football and fishing team trophies front and center in your first adult home.

"You ready to start the movie?" I smirk. I do my best charming when I'm insecure.

She laughs. "Sure, if you can call it that."

I take the flash drive from my pocket and put it in the TV. Ashley snuggles up on the couch, and I'd love nothing more than to rest my head against her shoulder and wrap my arm around her.

Instead, I settle for sitting a comfortable foot away and set the popcorn bowl between us.

The most interesting thing we find on the surveillance video is Paul stuffing a whole bucket of suckers in his pants pockets. Considering he's wearing painted-on Wranglers, that's quite a feat.

"Do you see some of this randomness that goes on?" I ask in between bites of popcorn.

"Some of it." Ashley laughs. "Paul's been known to steal suckers before, but I didn't realize he could stuff that many in those pants."

We both laugh. I reach for more popcorn and accidentally find her fingers in the bowl. She moves her hand, and I'm a little embarrassed.

Did I catch her off guard or is she that opposed to my touch?

I do what I do best and deflect. "What about Cynthia Gullsbee bringing that poodle in the bank?"

"That's been going on for months. She found some doctor online to sign off on Sprinkles being a service pet."

I frown. "Service for what?"

"Good question. I think that was her way of getting to take him anywhere she wants."

I shake my head. Some people will do anything to break and bend the law.

"The only rooms without a camera are Samuel's office and the back room?" I turn to her for clarification.

"Actually, Samuel's office has one. That view of the wall with golf trophies is his room."

I scoff. "What good is a stagnant camera pointed to the back wall?"

"Exactly." Ashley sighs.

"We need to plant some cameras."

She twists her lips. "Like in his office?"

I shake my head. "No, that's trespassing."

"Wasn't that what we did today?"

"Yeah, but nobody knows I was doing it." I steeple my hands and prop my chin on them to think. My mind wanders to places it probably shouldn't, but it leads me to a brilliant idea. I turn to Ashley and try not to stare at her shirt. "Are you okay with wearing a body mic?"

"Like an earpiece?"

"Yeah, and a mic to pick up conversations."

Her eyes widen. "Like going undercover?"

I waver my head. "You'd still be you, but have a hidden mic to capture conversations."

"Where would we put the mic?"

I look at her shirt.

Ashley blushes when she realizes I'm focusing on her chest. I open my mouth to apologize or make some lame excuse that under the collar is a common place to hide cameras. Luckily, we're interrupted by a loud boom against the front door. Ashley jumps toward me, and I wrap my arm around her without thinking.

"What was that?"

"I don't know, but I'll find out." I begrudgingly leave her side and open the door.

A large goat barrels through the room. It's that weird one with the pool noodles on its horns. He rushes toward my bookcase, butting his head. He rams the side of the built-ins, and my "Most Rushing Yards" plaque tumbles to the floor.

"Whoa." I set the plaque on the mantel and attempt to grab the goat by the horns.

I'm getting a hold on him when he snorts and runs. My grip slips, and I'm left standing with a broken pool noodle. Ashley has her legs hugged to her chest, terror in her eyes.

"Maybe we should call Daisy," she squeaks.

I wait for the demon to run my way and leap out in an attempt to tackle him. He's too fast, and I hit the hardwood floor with a splat.

"Hey, Daisy. Are you home?"

I manage to turn my face toward the couch. Ashley is scrunched in the corner with her phone against her ear. "Thanks," she says into the phone. She smiles at me nervously. "Help is on the way."

I drop my head and groan. My ribs tingle from the impact. I give myself a minute to regroup, then crawl back to the couch. I may not can save Ashley from this terror of a goat, but I can at least comfort her. We sit side by side, my arm around her for a glorious few minutes as we watch the goat use his noodle-free horn to shred my Bama throw pillow.

My heart tears with every shred. I've had that thing since college.

A loud whistle comes from the doorway. We both turn to Daisy and Kyle standing on the porch. The goat raises its head and snorts.

"I got this." Kyle walks calmly toward the beast and puts his hand on its neck. "Come on, Hoss. You've had enough fun for one night."

Hoss snorts as Kyle leads him toward the door. Daisy pets him between the horns, and his stubby tail wags.

"Here." I stand and hand them the broken pool noodle from the floor.

Daisy shakes her head. "Just as well. I need to put orange ones on him before hunting season anyway."

Kyle glances at Ashley, then makes eye contact with me. I clear my throat to silence him.

Unfortunately, Daisy isn't well versed in our secret language. "Hey, Ashley." She turns to me after Ashley greets her back. "Us four should double date sometime."

I freeze. All Ashley has to do is agree, and I'm all in.

Instead, she stands and goes toward the door. I look at Kyle, then Daisy, then Ashley, and back at Kyle. For the first time in my life, I'm speechless.

Daisy strokes Hoss's back. "We best get Hoss home. It was good seeing y'all. I'll be happy to pay for the pillow."

"It's fine, you can't really put a price on something old like that." I swallow. *Something I got my first week of pledging a fraternity.*

"I was just about to leave myself, actually," Ashley adds.

I follow everyone onto the porch and try to hide my disappointment. Did the double-date comment scare her off?

Kyle and Daisy walk toward her house with Hoss, and I walk Ashley to her car. I wait until they're out of earshot before I talk. "Think about the mic idea, but no pressure."

"I will." She smiles and climbs inside her car.

I bite my tongue before saying I'll call her. This is one girl

I don't want to ruin things with before they start. I'll let her call me.

Ashley

"Breathe in and lift." Daisy raises her nose to the air, and the rest of us follow.

I stare at her popcorn ceiling and hold my breath. She was brilliant to offer goat yoga on Mondays. Oddly, it's the perfect relaxation for the beginning of a work week.

Today was Samuel's first full day at work since he took off Thursday afternoon. He was in and out Friday and kept the back room on lockdown.

After the Monday morning rush, he gave me graphic details about Rambo's bowel issues. But he assured me the bunny made a full recovery, and then he didn't leave the bank once today. Not to grab lunch, meet with someone in the back, or anything. He stayed in his office all day, making me even more suspicious.

"Exhale, and bend at the waist."

I follow Daisy's instruction and drop my head between my shins. Tiny hooves scale up my back, offering a lumpy massage. I breathe gently and wait for the goat to dismount before raising my head. It trots toward Hannah and lets me be for a bit.

My mind wanders, playing out worst-case scenarios about Samuel and the bank. I haven't spoken to Bradley since Friday night after the goat break-in. He's probably waiting on my answer about a secret wire.

I hadn't thought about it until today when Samuel came back to work. My weekend was filled with shopping and trying to block out the awkwardness I showed Friday when I left.

I practically ran away after Daisy mentioned a double date. Why?

Because I'm scared of what Bradley would say, that's why. He's older and well-respected in the county. I'm in my early twenties, grew up in a rougher area, and have little viable skills other than processing a loan.

"Stand and lean to the right." Daisy's voice catches me off guard.

I only heard half of what she said, so I mimic the row in front of me. We shouldn't have much time left in this class.

So much for a relaxing night. Hopefully my body is refreshed, because my brain sure isn't.

She calls out several more poses in standing positions, then has us circle our arms overhead and bend forward. The blood rushes to my head, and I exhale to keep from falling.

At last she sends the goats away and turns down the lights. I lie on my back and take deep breaths. My eyes are still closed when Daisy raises the lights. I keep lying in silence long enough for most people to start gathering their mats.

"Here." Bianca slides a bottle of cleaner my way.

"Thanks." I wipe down my mat and carry it to the front.

A small group of regulars are gathered by the door, chatting with Daisy. They giggle when I join them.

That can't be good.

"Daisy was telling us about Hoss breaking in on y'all the other night," Adrianne says.

"Oh yeah." I fake laugh and hide my concern over what else Daisy said.

"Were you two on a date?" Carolina asks.

My limbs tingle. I want to run away from the awkwardness, but that would make things more awkward. So I freeze.

"We're friends," I finally say.

A collective moan comes from the group.

"What?"

Daisy frowns. "I was hoping you two were on a date."

So was I.

I shake my head.

"It looked like you were watching TV together."

"We were." I laugh nervously.

"That sounds like a date." Carolina wiggles her eyebrows.

I shift uncomfortably. Hannah is in front of the closed door, blocking my escape route.

"It looked boring too," Daisy says. "The perfect kind of TV for kissing."

Everyone laughs again.

"We really are just friends." I try and hide my disappointment.

"Friends watch boring, kiss-worthy TV together on a Friday night?" Adrianne cocks her head, calling my bluff.

"It was campaign videos. I'm helping him with his campaign."

"Oh." Bianca nods. "You'd be good at that."

"Thanks."

Great. Now I'm supposedly working on a campaign that doesn't exist. One that would put me even more at odds with Samuel.

I nod at the door. "I better get down the road. It's a decent drive home." Hannah moves to the side, and I open the door to make my escape.

"Ashley?" I half turn at Daisy's voice. "For what it's worth, we all think you two would make a good couple."

Everyone else nods or smiles in agreement. I give them a nervous wave and retreat to my car. While I'm flattered they approve of us—when at first many of them didn't even approve of me—there's too many other factors at play. I'm already anxious about spying on Samuel, yet I somehow managed to create a fake campaign.

Oh yay.

CHAPTER NINE

Bradley

Kyle stares at me fixing my baked potato.

"What?"

"No fries?" He frowns.

I shake my head.

"You always get fries."

"Thought I'd try my potatoes another way today."

"Are you trying to watch your weight?"

I scoff. "No." I drop my face and finish spreading the smallest bit of butter.

"You're into her, aren't you?"

I ignore Kyle, even though he's on to me. Anytime I think I might be shirtless in front of a woman, I cut back on fried foods.

"I'm talking about Ashley."

I stab my fork in my potato and give him a death glare.

"Dude, calm down."

I frown. "It's not that, or her. I've just got a lot going on."

"But you do *like* like her, right?"

"Here's that refill." The waitress brings Kyle another tea.

"Thanks." He smiles at her before staring at me sternly.

"Why are you so interested in my love life?" I shove a forkful of potato in my mouth and pretend it's Mary's crispy fries instead.

"It doesn't matter much now that I know you two weren't on a date. I just thought I sensed something between you."

"When did you get so sensitive and start sensing things?"

"I'm not sensitive." His voice is defensive and makes me smirk. "You look at her the way I look at Daisy is all."

I take a big gulp of my drink. I've always been a flirt, so for Kyle to notice something extra in the way I look at Ashley . . . she could notice it too.

He runs his fry through a pile of ketchup and tosses it in his mouth. I'm a little jealous. Not just of the fries, but because he's found his person.

Even if Ashley does notice how I feel, I can't act on it right now.

"It's cool. Your secret's safe with me." Kyle grins as he bites into his burger.

I chew a piece of grilled chicken and pretend it's fried. We eat in silence a few more minutes before he speaks. "Besides, Daisy told me you two were there to work on your campaign."

I choke on a piece of chicken and take a big swallow of my drink to wash it down.

"You okay?" Kyle looks mildly worried.

I nod and cough it off. "Yeah."

I just wasn't aware I had a campaign. I've put signs all over the county, including some at the county line and a billboard on a trailer downtown. What more is there to do?

"Maybe you should tell her how you feel. Don't wait for her to go to Waffle House with some other guy."

"Kyle, I'm not you, big dog."

"I know." He continues eating.

I drown a piece of chicken in ranch and consider Ashley running a campaign. I'm not sure how that rumor got started, but it doesn't much matter now.

A lot of rumors start at the hair salon. Hair dryers blowing make women think they hear one thing, then they run with it. That's probably the case. I just suspected it to take longer than a few days. I blame Daisy.

It doesn't help that she's best friends with the salon owner.

"I can't believe that Hopper guy is running against you."

That makes two of us. "I guess I got lucky last time, running unopposed after the long-time sheriff decided to retire."

"Everyone loves you, Bradley. You'll be fine."

I sure hope so. A campaign manager is starting to sound like a smart idea, especially if she's blonde with long legs.

"Thanks, man." I leave it at that to hide any fear I have of losing.

It works, because Kyle starts to talk about his two favorite subjects—football and engines. And I'm ninety-nine percent sure he can't circle those back to Ashley. We eat the rest of our lunch discussing the SEC and Wisteria's recent win over Apple Cart. I almost forget about the campaign rumor and the fact that someone is running against me.

Until I go to the counter to pay. Becki Douglas, who runs the county newspaper, is there picking up a to go order. She pays Mary, then smiles at me when she turns around. "Bradley Manning. I was planning on calling you this week."

"You were?" We've never been each other's type, so she must need a quote for a story.

"I want to host a debate between you and Vernon Hopper."

My eyes widen. "Debate?"

"Yes. It's the first time we've had more than one candidate run for sheriff in years."

"Okay?"

"Come on, it'll be fun." She punches my arm lightly. "This will be great local news."

"Might as well," Mary chimes in from behind the counter. "Ashley can coach you as your campaign manager."

I raise my brow at her. "How did—" I shake my head. "Never mind."

Mary winks at me. She has some sort of sixth sense about everything going on with everybody in town.

"I'll get you details ASAP." Becki smiles, then turns on her heel and marches out of the restaurant.

"Eight sixty-three, sugar," Mary says behind me.

I turn from watching Becki and pull out my wallet. So much for a peaceful lunch with a friend. All I wanted was a baked potato, and instead I got a campaign and a debate. At least I can't complain about my campaign manager.

Ashley

My phone buzzes against my desk. I push it away and continue working on the loan reports. I've worked nonstop, barely taking a lunch break. Apparently, Tuesday is the new Monday this week.

When I finish one set of files, I break to check my phone.

It's a text from Bradley. My face involuntarily curves into a big smile. Then it quickly straightens when I read the message.

Heard you're my campaign manager.

My stomach cramps. I'm an idiot for making that up, especially in front of a group of women. Especially when the group includes the owner of Cut and Dry, Apple Cart's hub of fake news and gossip.

I tap my thumbnail against the phone, mentally preparing my response.

"Ashley?"

I drop the phone in my lap and turn to Samuel walking toward me. He comes and sits on the edge of my desk.

"Ashley, I want to apologize for having you make all those copies."

My phone slides down my skirt to the floor. Samuel has never apologized to me for anything. "Thanks?"

"What are you working on now?" He leans closer to my computer.

"Processing loans."

He nods. "When you finish that, come by my office. I need your help with something important."

I raise my brows. He smiles, then heads down the hall. Confused, I watch him retreat to his office.

The stack of loans calls to me, and I continue working. Samuel apologizing for belittling me almost makes up for the fact that I lied about running Bradley's campaign. I just hate that he found out through the rumor mill before I had a chance to explain.

Half an hour later, I shut down my computer and stand

in front of Samuel's office. My fingers shake before I make a fist and knock on his door. I'm both excited and a little worried about whatever he has for me. You never know with Samuel.

"Come in."

I let myself in, and he stands before I cross the room. He meets me halfway and puts his hand on my back. I stall, allowing him to walk ahead of me so his hand naturally falls away. We leave his office and cross the hall to the forbidden back room. He pulls a key from his pocket and unlocks the door.

My pulse races. Does he somehow know I've been in here? Did he leave the door cracked last week as a test? This feels like a trap. Not the usual trap I find myself in where someone from high school sends me a messenger request wanting to sell face cream. The kind of trap you see in movies where you enter a room and never come out.

The green computer screen glows inside the dark room when he opens the door. I try and look surprised at the odd mixture of papers and vintage electronics.

Samuel flips on the light, and I blink to adjust my eyes. "This is the back room," he says, shutting the door.

Now it really feels like a trap.

"We file all the special loans here."

"Special loans?"

He smiles. "Yeah, the kind that are worth a certain amount of money or need rushed."

A lump forms in my throat. This is not good. Fortunately, I have a hidden talent. I can play convincingly naive. "Why is this computer all black and green?"

"It's a different brand."

"What about this apple?" I run my hand across the front below the screen.

"No, see, it says Macintosh." Samuel's voice is so condescending, I want to punch him.

"Ohhh." I channel my anger into acting extra clueless.

"Now, I brought you in here to show you that the copies I had you make were not just to keep you busy. They are very important files."

I nod and smile like I'm in a pageant interview.

"I know I can trust you to realize their importance and to help me copy more, right?"

I nod and smile again, though I'm scowling inside. Just when I thought I'd get out of making copies.

Samuel walks me to the files we found earlier, and I act as if this is all new to me. He shows me the boxes and explains how I can get them to copy, then put them back. He then shows me an old copier in the corner so that I don't have to go in the copy room.

When I can hardly stand his overexplaining anymore, he does something I never expected. He hands me the key to the room. The silver object glistens against the green computer and overhead florescent lighting.

I wrap my hand around it and stare at him. "Don't you need the key?"

"I have another one in my office."

I lift my chin. How many more keys are there to this room? I decide not to ask and let him do all the talking.

"Whenever you're not busy, I want you to come back here and make copies until all those boxes have ten copies."

My eyes run together as I scan the shelf full of boxes. I start to ask why not Glenda. Then it hits me. Samuel thinks she might get suspicious. He either thinks I'm too naive to realize these loans are bogus or that I'll go along with whatever he says. Either way, I'm offended.

However, I play along and keep smiling. "Okay, I'll come back after I send a few emails."

"Good deal." He heads toward the door, then turns. "And keep the door locked at all times. There is top-secret info in here."

"Will do." I leave the room and narrow my eyes as he crosses the hall and shuts himself in his office. Then I lock the back-room door and hurry to my desk. It's safe to say I have a response for Bradley.

I retrieve my phone from the floor and open my text. My hand hovers over the keyboard before I type something about Samuel. We don't need a message trail on this. Good thing I've thought of the perfect code word. I just didn't realize it until now.

Yep, I've got some ideas and more info for your campaign. Talk later.

CHAPTER TEN

Bradley

I'm elbows deep in a bag of Doritos while binge watching *NCIS: New Orleans* when someone knocks on my door. I jolt out of my cop-show coma and wipe cheese dust down the crusty T-shirt I've had since football. "Wisteria Mud Cats" is barely legible with all the tears and fading this shirt has endured for a little more than a decade.

I lick my fingertips on my way to the door, wondering who it could be. Clearly, I'm not expecting anyone.

My nerves fire on all cylinders when I open the door to Ashley. She gives me a quick glance, then surprisingly smiles.

"Come in." I move aside and attempt to smooth out the permanent wrinkles in my shirt. "I apologize for my appearance."

She smiles wider. "Never. It's nice to see that Bradley Manning is human."

That makes me grin. I hurry to the couch and dust off

the Doritos crumbs. This is why I need to eat a more filling lunch. It always comes back to bite me later.

Ashley sits on the opposite end of the couch from the chips, and I don't blame her. I sit in my mess and forget my shirt also has sleeveless armholes cut deep down the sides until I lay my arm across the couch.

"I should've called, but I came right after work."

"No, it's fine." *Although a little heads-up would've been nice.*

She lifts her hands and sighs. The way her bracelets twirl around her tiny wrists is endearing. And also a slap in the face to how underdressed I am compared to her.

"First off, I apologize about the campaign rumor. I accidentally started that at goat yoga yesterday."

"How?"

"Daisy mentioned the goat thing Friday night and us watching TV together. I panicked and said we were watching campaign videos for ideas."

I burst out laughing.

"What?" Ashley laughs too, making me laugh harder. "It's all I could think of. Daisy put me on the spot saying that we were watching some boring TV perfect for making out."

I stop laughing and hold my breath. Fire shoots up my spine like an electrical current as I focus on Ashley's lips. Her full, pink, perfectly kissable lips.

Would she consider *NCIS* a make-out show?

Ashley clears her throat, alerting me that I've stared at her an uncomfortable amount of time. I lift my eyes to hers, which isn't much safer. They're blue pools I wish I could fall into and never come up for air. I'd gladly drown in them.

"Are you mad?" She winces.

"Huh? Oh. No!" *Darn it, Bradley.* "I'm not mad at all. It's not the first time Daisy's said something that's shocked me."

She smirks, and the cutest little laugh seeps out. It takes

all my willpower to not kiss her right now. And since I'm wearing ratty sweats covered in Doritos crumbs, it's safe to say my willpower is at an all-time low.

"Good, because a campaign was the first thing I could think of to convince them we weren't on a date."

My ego deflates like a whoopee cushion. *What's so bad about the two of us on a date?*

I dismiss that thought and try to salvage what little self-respect I have left. "You know, Ashley, a campaign isn't so unbelievable with Hopper putting up signs around town."

She perks up. "Really?"

I smile at having helped erase her worry.

"I've never ran a campaign before, but if you do need help . . ." She pauses and takes a deep breath.

"If I need help with anything besides signs, you'll be my first call. But I was more so thinking it's a brilliant cover-up for us to meet together about the Samuel stuff."

"Brilliant?"

I nod and her face lights up.

"It does make me a little nervous when I have to sneak around Samuel to call or text you."

I grit my teeth at the thought of Samuel snooping on Ashley's private life. Of course, we're doing that to him, but it's to protect society.

"We need some kind of code," she suggests.

She twists her lips and stares at the ceiling. I study her cuteness, then look away when her eyes meet mine. "How about a safe word—or emoji—to text?" I suggest.

Her eyes light up. "Like something I can text you when we need to talk?"

"Yeah. That way you won't have to worry about texting details and saying them over the phone while at work." I glance across the room and spot my hat resting on the arm of a chair. "How about the cowboy smiley emoji?"

She laughs. Maybe I should've gone with something a little less comical.

"I love it."

My chest tightens at the word "love" leaving her lips. She means it in a very nonchalant way, but she said it, and she said it to me.

"Anyway, now that we've cleared up the campaign stuff . . ." She winks.

My heart skips an unhealthy number of beats.

"Samuel introduced me to the back room today."

"Oh." I sit up straighter and blink.

"Yeah, I'm afraid he may try and use me as an accomplice or something."

"No wonder you're scared to call me at work."

"Either he thinks I'm too dense to know what's going on, or he thinks I'll go along with anything he does. Either is an insult." She huffs.

I scoot a little closer. "Ashley, don't worry about what he thinks. He's wrong."

She half smiles. We share a look for a few seconds before she pulls something from her purse. "I got today's footage, but I'm certain there's no camera in the back room. And the one in his office stays in the same location, getting the back wall only."

I steeple my fingers and rest them under my chin. "I hate to ask this of you, but are you comfortable with me wiring you?"

She sucks in a breath, then exhales. "Do you think I can do it right?"

"Absolutely. All I need is for you to have the recording on when you're around Samuel."

I reach out and grab her hand. It's tiny, warm, and comforting. "You can do anything you want, Ashley. I want to make sure you're comfortable, is all. I'd never want to do anything that might cause you harm."

Her hand curls inside mine and we share a brief moment. I inch closer. She moves her hand and replaces it with the flash drive, then jumps to her feet. "Thanks, Bradley. I better go."

"You're welcome?" I mumble as she lets herself out.

"We'll talk soon," she says, halfway out the door.

I point her way. "Cowboy emoji."

She shuts the door, and I drop my head in my hands. "Cowboy emoji? I'm such a dork."

Ashley

The clock on the wall ticks by another minute, announcing that it's closing time.

Bonnie starts counting down the drawers with her tellers, and Glenda pulls the shades down at the drive-through. I push away from my desk and walk to the front door. If I don't lock it, someone will slide in and want help. And it's always for something simple they can do via the drop box or our website. However, Apple Cart has a whole generation who choose to boycott anything but face-to-face banking.

Speaking of such, there's one customer left. I set the door to lock from the outside and focus on the kiosk in the center of the lobby. Paul is strategically hidden behind the wall of pamphlets and deposit slips, only visible from the door.

"Paul?"

He jerks around, dropping about twenty suckers in the process.

"We're closing. Did you need help with something?"

I struggle to keep a polite tone since I watched a teller help him half an hour ago. Has he stood there this long?

"Could you help me find some of those blue raspberry suckers?"

I sigh. "I see about five by your boots."

He stares at the floor, then bends to pick one up. "I thought that was cotton candy."

"No, sir. Those also have pink on the wrapper."

"Ah." He squats and scans the floor for every dark blue wrapped sucker he can find with the patience and care of a kindergarten teacher checking a kid's scalp for lice.

When he has a fistful, he stands. I squint at the sunlight reflecting from his huge belt buckle. He nods and smiles, then struts out the door.

What he didn't do was pick up the suckers that aren't blue raspberry. I bend and gather them, then add them to the bucket on the kiosk.

Whistling echoes from the other side of the lobby and I stiffen. Samuel.

He never whistles unless he's alone, which means Glenda and Bonnie are gone. I can't exit through the back like everyone else, or he will see me. My only option is the front door.

I swallow and plan my escape. When the whistling dies down, I take a big step toward the door.

"Ashley."

Ughhh. I grit my teeth and freeze.

He catches up to me and puts his hand on my shoulder. I cringe and slowly turn. Thankfully, he moves his hand when I face him.

"I'm glad I caught you. Could you do some things for me since you're still here?"

I open my mouth, but nothing comes out.

"Good. It won't take long. Come with me."

Half out of fear and half out of shock, I follow him.

To the back room.

My stomach churns as he takes down a box from the collection and explains that he needs me to skip to this one. I feign interest, then pull my phone from my skirt pocket once he leaves. With shaky fingers, I unlock my phone and send the cowboy smiley emoji to Bradley. I lean against the block wall and take a deep breath as I stare at my screen. When he doesn't text right back, I open the box and pull the first page from the top.

It's a personal loan taken out by Diesel, who manages Piggly Wiggly. I've been in town longer than him, and he's never come in for a loan. I shake my head and make eleven copies. One will go in my pocket to show Bradley.

He's barely left my mind when sirens scream outside the bank. I push a box closer to the tiny back window and stand on it to look outside. I can't see anything but trees and grass.

By the time I make it down the hallway, Bradley and Samuel are in the lobby. I take in the view of them facing off across the tile floor with the sun setting behind them. Bradley's hands are on his hips, and Samuel is maybe a foot away with crossed arms, his gold watch on full display.

I size them up apples to oranges, and Bradley wins in every way possible. Attitude, appearance, personality.

The only thing Samuel might have on him is money, which, in the words of the great philosopher Shania Twain: "That don't impress me much."

Once I bore of assessing their stare down, I walk toward them and speak. "What's going on?"

Samuel's eyes widen as if he's shocked to see me. "Ashley, I thought you were working."

"I was, until I heard sirens."

He slants his eyes at Bradley. "Sherriff Manning got a call that some suspicious activity was going on here."

"Really?" I feign shock.

Bradley sneaks a quick smirk my way, then straightens his face when Samuel clears his throat. "Everything up here looks clear. Should I check the back?"

"No!" Samuel yells, causing Bradley to flinch.

My eyes widen, and Samuel chuckles nervously. "I mean, no use in wasting your time. We were the only ones back there, and I didn't hear anything." He turns to me. "I assume Ashley didn't either."

I glance between the two of them, unsure of how to answer.

"I think Ashley can go on home just to be safe, and I'll lock everything up," Samuel says.

"I'd be happy to wait here or go with you to secure everything," Bradley offers.

"No." Samuel adds another chuckle to not sound so aggressive.

"Then I'll escort Miss Ashley out to keep her safe."

Samuel opens his mouth, but quickly closes it. Bradley has him in a tough spot. If he says I need to stay, it will make him look suspicious or raise questions of why I'm in the back.

Very well played, Sherriff Manning.

"That's very considerate of you." I smile at Bradley. "I'll go get my things, and Samuel can close out my extra workspace." I tighten my lips and glance at Samuel.

His face is blank, as if he's still contemplating a response to how all this is playing out.

I cross the floor and gather my purse and sweater from

my desk. Then I push in my chair and stand beside Bradley. "I'm ready."

He nods, then follows me to the front exit. He holds the door open and calls, "Good evening," to Samuel.

I don't look back until I'm at my car. "That wasn't exactly how I expected you to react to the emoji."

Bradley grins. "I was close by and didn't want to chance anything."

"Well, thank you."

"Anytime."

I turn my head toward the bank to Samuel staring at us. Bradley follows my gaze and frowns. "Let's start driving, and I'll follow you out," he whispers near my ear.

I nod and open my car door.

Samuel stands at the bank entrance, arms folded, a huge scowl covering his face. I back out of the parking lot and roll my eyes. Then I watch Bradley pull behind my car.

Thank God for the cowboy smiley emoji. It's like having my own personal superhero on call.

CHAPTER ELEVEN

Bradley

I planned to drive about a mile past the bank, then go back to the sheriff's office. But what if Samuel drives by and sees my car?

What if he drives anywhere in Apple Cart County and sees my car? It takes time to get to Sparrow. He would know I wouldn't have had time to follow Ashley home and get back in less than an hour.

That's the excuse I use to justify following her all the way home.

I've driven her home once before. Ironically, when I offered her a ride home from goat yoga after Samuel left mad. Ever since, I've wanted a reason to come back, to meet her family and see how she lives.

The woman intrigues me.

She parks her small car in the drive, and I pull my cop

car behind her. We both get out, and she turns to me. "You didn't have to follow me all the way here."

My mouth tries to smile, but I keep a serious face. "I wanted to make sure Samuel wouldn't follow you and try something funny."

"I appreciate it." She lowers her face, then lifts it to reveal blushing cheeks. "And I appreciate you coming to check on me so quickly after the text."

"No problem. Cowboy Smiley at your service." I salute her, and she laughs.

"What's going on?"

I glance over Ashley's shoulder to an older version of her walking toward us. When she's fully in the garage light, I see the concern in her eyes. She stares at my car, then my badge. "I thought I saw a cop car, but I couldn't leave the stove."

Ashley frowns. "What if it had been a real emergency?"

"Oh, Ashley. You know I wouldn't leave you to die. Nor would I leave your dad to burn down the kitchen."

Ashley shakes her head. "Bradley, meet my mother, Connie."

I extend my hand. "Mrs. Armstrong, nice to meet you."

"You as well. Call me Connie so I won't feel as old." She shakes my hand, then sighs. "Is something wrong?" She scans me head to toe, then fixes her eyes on the cop car.

"No, ma'am."

"Nothing's wrong. Bradley followed me home after an odd call at the bank," Ashley adds.

Her face softens after Ashley's reassurance. "Would you like to stay for supper?" She smiles.

Ashley's mouth parts, and she looks to me for an answer.

"If it's all right with Ashley, but I'd hate to impose."

With the help of overhead light, I can see Ashley blushing more. "It's good with me," she says.

I follow the two of them inside to a pristinely kept living room. Ashley's dad sits in the corner reading a newspaper. It's all very *Leave It to Beaver*, but with modern furniture and clothing.

He lowers the paper when I shut the door behind us.

"Honey, this is Bradley. He will be joining us for supper."

He stands, and I calculate that he has at least two inches on me. That's got to be where Ashley gets such long legs.

"So that was the commotion outside."

I ball my hand in a fist, suddenly too intimidated to greet him.

"Bradley followed me home. There was a warning call about something going on at the bank."

"I see." He adjusts his belt and stands straighter.

"Your wife invited me to stay. I don't have to if it's a problem."

He shakes his head. "Fine by me as long as you don't eat more than your share."

A lump forms in my throat as I mentally calculate what a fair share would be for someone my age and stature.

"He's kidding." Ashley places her hand on my elbow. My internal tension dies down as she keeps her hand there halfway to the kitchen.

That room is like *Southern Living* with sarcasm. Every wall has a framed quote or quirky saying. My favorite is the one explaining how macaroni and cheese is a vegetable in the South. Anyone who's eaten at Mary's Diner would have to agree.

I start to pull out Ashley's chair, but glance at her dad. I need to at least properly meet him first, and properly find out if she wants me to do date-ish things like pull out her chair.

"I don't believe we've properly met, sir. I'm Bradley Manning." I hold out my hand.

He shakes it firmly. "Ernie. Nice to meet you."

If there's one thing I learned watching *The Office*, it's

never be the first to break a handshake. Mr. Armstrong must be a Dwight fan himself, since we continue this for at least a minute. He loosens his grip at last, giving me freedom to do so as well.

"Nice firm handshake." He turns to Ashley. "Much preferred to the guy with the pet rabbit and overweight Rolex."

Ashley's nostrils flare a bit. I bite my tongue to keep from laughing. I take it Mr. Armstrong isn't a fan of Samuel, same as most people.

Connie enters with a platter of potatoes and sets them beside the roast chicken and green beans already on the table. I glance at my plate, then Mr. Armstrong. I won't dare call him Ernie, unless he offers.

He's staring at my hat. I slowly remove it and set it by my feet. Satisfied, he turns his attention to the chicken. "I'll say grace."

As Ernie prays, I bow my head, but run a hand over my hair. I hate when I can't check for hat hair. I imagine a dorky hat ring outlining my forehead.

Ashley smiles at me after the "amen," easing my nerves a little.

We fill our plates as Connie asks what we'd like to drink. I choose water, since I don't want to be judged for drinking too much caffeine. I'm still recovering from Ernie's dry-humored comment about how much I should eat.

"Bradley, how long have you been a sheriff?" Connie asks.

"Almost four years." I take a sip of water and clear my throat. "I have to run for reelection this term."

She nods. "I think it's sweet how Ashley is helping with your campaign."

Ashley squeezes my knee under the table, and every hair

on my neck stands to attention. I almost choke on my chicken.

"Sorry," she mouths in a hushed voice after I look her way.

I take a gulp of water, all too aware that her hand is still on my leg. She slides it away gently, and the neck hairs lay down one at a time.

If we ever do get together, I hope to one day ask her if she was sorry for mentioning the campaign or for almost making me choke.

I half smile at Connie and send up a silent prayer that she doesn't ask me anything about the campaign I don't know anything about. Ashley told me she told people I have one, but she hasn't given me any details.

"The first time I ever saw Connie, she was working the poll."

Now I do choke on my water.

"She was so beautiful," Ernie continues.

"I wasn't actually working, since I was still underage."

I cough, and Ashley slaps my back. My eyes water, and I bury my head in my hands. She had mentioned her mom used to be a dancer, but I never suspected she worked for Sparrow Booby Trap.

"My grandma worked there every year and always talked about how fun it was. She said I could go learn when I was a teenager."

I cough again.

"Up until she died, my great-grandma still went in and checked IDs and handed out stickers." Ashley smiles proudly.

"Stickers?" *What in the heck would those say, "I got caught at Sparrow Booby Trap"?*

"Yeah, the little flags that say, 'I voted.'"

My jaw drops with realization, and my body drops about ten pounds of stress with it. "The election poll."

"Yeah, what did you think we were talking about?" Ashley laughs.

I fan a hand dismissively. All eyes are on me. "This is good chicken."

"Well, thank you. My grandma taught me that too."

I nod and stuff some potatoes in my face. We eat in silence for a few seconds, and this time I'm thankful the conversation shifts back to me.

"What made you want to be sheriff?" Ernie's eyebrows pinch together, making him look more like a Bert.

"I got a degree in criminal justice. I was going to work for the government or CIA, or something grand, but I missed home."

Sweat beads on my neck. That probably makes me sound like someone who gave up and took the easy road. But it's the truth. I did miss home.

I moved back and messed up the one real relationship I've ever had, the one woman I'd loved, who loved the city too much to make us work. I haven't felt anything close for anyone since.

Until Ashley.

I glance at her and pretend we're a couple for a brief second. I'm lost in her lovely face when her dad calls my attention.

"There's nothing wrong with that."

My neck sweat simmers down and I relax in my seat.

"I had no interest in my dad's auto-parts store until I went to college. Then I couldn't wait to move back."

Did we just semi-bond over something? I'm starting to like this man, and I think he may like me too. And now that I know his wife isn't a former underage pole dancer, I can enjoy the conversation.

We talk more about random topics, including the

weather and football season. Everything is going smoothly until ol' Ernie throws me a curveball.

"Bradley, do you play table tennis?"

Ashley

"If you're referring to ping-pong, I've played before," Bradley answers calmly.

I fight rolling my eyes at Daddy's question. He loves sports of any kind. Despite his efforts, the closest thing to a racket or bat I swung was a baton. My younger sister, Katherine, followed Mama as a ballerina. So anytime a guy comes around, he finds an opportunity for competitive camaraderie.

I toy with the bracelets on my wrist in anticipation of the impending showdown. Mama sighs when we enter the rec room. I'm certain she's dealt with Daddy's male competitiveness more than any of us.

My dad's family was big on recreational-type skills. Even in his fifties, he can roller skate backward and double-under with a jump rope.

Bradley stops at the edge of the table while Mama takes a seat in the corner. Daddy hands Bradley a paddle, and he thanks him. Then he swaps it to his left hand.

I find this interesting since I've only seen him use his right hand for utensils and writing tools. Maybe he's one of those people who has a different dominant hand for sports, like a switch hitter. I shrug and take a seat by Mama on our old couch. It's a little like déjà vu of the time Daddy challenged—and beat—Samuel at darts. Katherine's current boyfriend played him in cornhole.

How he decides which challenge for which guy shall remain a mystery, but he loves a good matchup. When a game gets close, he's like an overly dominant dog ready to pee on anything threatening to cross his territory.

Bradley stands patiently as Daddy lays out the rules. He gives Bradley the first serve, and the game is in motion.

Mama loses interest and fidgets with fluffing the cushions on the couch. I move to the edge to get a better view . . . and because she's now fluffing the pillows behind me.

Daddy and Bradley go back and forth, making it resemble a live-action pong game. Most people don't keep up with him this long at any activity. And it shows when he steps back and wipes sweat from his brow. They're tied, and Bradley gives me a wink. My heart skips a beat. I smile to discreetly encourage him.

After another quick break to wipe his brow and roll up his sleeves, Daddy serves. They go back and forth so much that even Mama looks up from picking at her nails. This lasts at least ten minutes and feels like ten hundred.

Bradley's ball lands in the corner, making it hard for Daddy to hit it back. He swings, but misses just in time for his smartwatch to beep. Mama gasps.

He'd set an alarm for when the game would end. On the rare occasion a game lasted until the buzzer, he would be way ahead. In all my twenty-three years, I've yet to see him lose.

Until now.

As if that weren't shocking enough, Daddy does something totally out of character. He crosses the table to Bradley's side and extends a hand. Bradley stares at it a beat, then shakes it.

"Good game, son." Daddy smiles.

A thin smile slides up Bradley's cheeks, as if his brain has to convince his face it's okay to relax. "Thanks. You too, sir."

"Call me Ernie."

I almost pass out. He rarely offers that to anyone under thirty, especially someone he just met.

Mama blinks away the shock, then stands. "Would anyone like some pie?" she asks.

Daddy and Bradley both agree, and I follow behind everyone to the living room. A few minutes later, we're seated around the coffee table eating apple pie.

"This is delicious, Mrs. Armstrong."

"Please, it's Connie," Mama corrects Bradley. "And it is delicious, but I didn't make it."

"I did," Daddy says.

I frown at him.

"I made it by buying it at the bakery in Apple Cart." He chuckles.

This time I do roll my eyes. If the dad jokes are out, he's in a good mood. Mama smiles at me in between bites.

For the next half hour, Daddy asks Bradley about his job and hobbies. They continue the dinner discussions of football, the weather, and what guns he prefers for hunting. It's not unusual for him to grill a guy upon meeting him. But it is unusual for him to smile and laugh while doing it.

Either the apple orchard snuck something illegal in this pie, or Daddy actually likes Bradley. Of course, most people like Bradley. Older people, kids, pets . . . and me.

Bradley straightens his hat and sets his empty plate on the coffee table. He nods at my parents. "Thank you both for the hospitality." He turns to my dad. "And for the recreation. I best be on my way." He stands and shakes my dad's hand once more.

"I'll walk you out," I say without thinking.

Neither of my parents protests. Not that they should,

given my age and how they're practically drooling over Bradley.

I flip on the porch light and follow him outside. A breeze whips through and chills my arms. I wipe my hands up and down my thin sleeves to try and warm myself. Then a strong, warm hand lands on my shoulder.

Bradley hugs me close to his side. My body tingles as I lean into his warmth. We walk linked together to his car. It's so comforting that I wish we had a longer walkway. Instead, we're by his door in under a minute.

My heart beats faster as he slides his arm from around my shoulders and faces me. If this hadn't felt like a date before, it sure does now. A thousand questions circle in my mind when he leans closer.

I swallow and stare at his mouth. Would he try to kiss me?

He does—on the cheek.

That's cool. Totally appropriate. But it does leave me to wonder if he wants it to be more one day. I sure do.

"Thanks again for inviting me in. Your family is great."

"You haven't met my younger sister yet." My cheeks flush. I tend to say something random when I'm nervous.

"I'm sure she's great too." Bradley smiles and reaches for his door, then shades his eyes. Headlights blind us in the driveway.

My sister's boyfriend parks his truck, and they get out. "Well, here she is."

Before I can introduce Bradley to Katherine, Trey runs toward us with eyes as wide as bottle tops. He raises his palms. "I swear, whatever you heard is not true. I did not participate in the paintball fight at Broken Bridge."

Bradley laughs. "Whatever you say, big dog." Then he gives Trey a stern glare. "But I'll be watching you."

"Yes sir." Trey grabs Katherine's hand, and they rush in the house.

I laugh. "And that's her boyfriend."

"I assumed."

"Be careful." I smile.

Bradley gets in his car and smiles back. "Always." He winks and rolls up his window.

I stand and watch until he's out of sight. The wind picks up even harder, but somehow, I'm no longer cold.

CHAPTER TWELVE

Ashley

A waterfall of suckers cascades down my desk and rolls across the lobby floor.

I sigh and crane my neck to make sure Samuel is still in the back. Thank goodness Bonnie is working the drive-through window, or I'd be stuck here alone with him.

Saturdays aren't too busy during football season, so it wouldn't be uncommon for Samuel to give everyone the day off. Except for me.

I stand and begin picking up my mess. A tower of suckers is not so sturdy, but it made for a nice distraction until we can leave.

"I'll take those." I lift my eyes to Paul squatted in front of me, grinning like a possum. Normally, I'd try and limit him, but it will help me out. As an added bonus, I'm pretty sure they're nearing expiration.

"Okay." I rock back on my heels and stand.

Paul's grin morphs into a wide smile as he stuffs his pockets. I'm slightly amazed at how many suckers fit in those tight Wranglers.

"Did you need anything, Paul, besides a month's worth of suckers?"

He chuckles and adjusts his belt buckle. His pockets bulge like a chipmunk's cheeks. Not a good look for anyone.

"I need to get some cash."

"Okay." I walk to the nearest teller station and motion for him to follow. "How much? And your business or personal account?"

"Three hundred, personal account, and put it in singles."

"All ones?" I wince, hoping he doesn't elaborate too much with his answer.

"Yep." He leans closer and whispers, "Don't rat me out to the preacher, but Dot and me are going to Tunica tonight."

I sigh with relief. My mind went to a darker scenario that didn't involve Dot. "I'll have to go in the vault for that many ones, hang on."

Paul turns his back to the counter and opens a sucker as I unlock the vault. My eyes meet the camera in the corner and an eeriness looms over me. I'm not doing anything wrong or out of the ordinary. But it has me wondering if anyone else has been today. Samuel spent a good thirty minutes in here this morning. That's a long time to stay in a small room without a toilet.

Images of Samuel messing with the camera or hiding something in an empty safe deposit box makes it hard to breathe. I retrieve the stacks of ones and get out of there as soon as possible. Never have I welcomed the overly air-conditioned lobby more. I exhale and return to the teller station.

Paul casually turns as he bites into a sucker.

I take my time counting the ones, which we have paper-clipped into stacks of twenty-five. At least that's what they're supposed to be.

All these check out as the right amount. But I can't quite shake the image of Samuel shorting every stack of ones by one. Like how the dude on that *Office Space* movie stole parts of pennies.

To my relief, everything checks out. I grab a manila envelope to hold it all before the bills tumble like my sucker stack. "Here you go."

"Thank you, ma'am." Paul straightens from leaning against the counter and takes the envelope.

I finish coding in the withdrawal and hand him a receipt. He smiles and takes another bite of his sucker. "If we strike it big, I'll bring you back a souvenir."

"Thank you." I try not to laugh when I smile back. I'm not very optimistic about anyone striking it rich at the Mississippi casinos, especially Paul and Dot. And on the off chance that they do, whatever souvenir he brings home will be odd and useless.

Paul waves the envelope and struts toward the door. I lower my head and discover a soggy sucker stick on the counter. Snarling, I go to the closet for cleaning supplies.

Samuel meets me in the hallway and grabs my elbow. "Shouldn't you be out front for customers?"

My eyes widen, and I glance at his hand. He lets go and takes a step back.

"Bonnie is out front. I'm getting something to clean the counter."

He frowns but nods. I hurry past him and try not to think of why he's so protective of the back area today. Maybe it's all in my head.

I return with Clorox wipes and focus on scrubbing all the sticky Paul-ness off the quartz surface. Then I turn around and gasp. Samuel is standing maybe a foot behind me. Is he a ninja now?

He clears his throat and grins. "I meant to ask if you'd like to join me for dinner tonight."

No, absolutely no. The last thing I need is to give him any false hope of us being on a date.

"Not catfish this time. Dinner at my house."

"I don't think we should date." I frown in an effort to prove I'm not joking.

His face flattens. "Oh, I didn't mean to offend you. This is more of a business dinner."

"Then why not just lunch?" I raise my brow in question.

"I've been wanting to use my Big Green Egg." He shrugs. "And Rambo really misses you."

I sigh. That dang rabbit. Samuel knows I have a soft spot for it.

"I can pick you up if you're worried about wasting gas."

A laugh sneaks out of me. Of all the odd arguments to convince me to eat with him. "I think I can manage."

His lips curve into a slight grin. "How about you come by around seven?"

"That will work."

He reaches toward me, and I follow his hand with my eyes. Instead of touching me, he taps the counter beside me, then hurries toward the back.

Bonnie meets my eyes and gives me a confused look. I shrug and roll my eyes. She laughs.

I can't tell if Samuel wants to date me or simply wants me to want him to date me. Regardless, I need some advice before spending time alone with him. Especially if he plans to bring up work. What if he confides in me about something illegal? Or worse, asks for my help?

Every hair on my arms stands up.

I rush to my desk for my phone. Then I text the cowboy emoji to Bradley, in hopes he can give advice on Samuel.

My phone buzzes and the response appears. A pig emoji followed by the number one.

I text a question mark.

Pig at 1 p.m.

That, I understand. I give him a thumbs-up and shove my phone in my purse. Now if only I can quit worrying until then.

At one on the dot, I park in front of Piggly Wiggly. I see Bradley's truck, but he isn't in it. I scan the parking lot, then decide to go in the store.

My phone dings, and I get a corncob emoji. Very strange.

Not that I expect Bradley to be so forward, but I sincerely hope this isn't some kind of redneck euphemism.

"Psst. Ashley."

I jerk my head toward the whisper-yell to see Bradley standing behind a bin of corn. He waves me over with a cob in his hand.

"Hey."

"I'm trying to catch some teenagers who've been stealing corncobs."

"Why?"

"To stop them."

I laugh. "No, why would anyone steal corn?"

"They like to throw the kernels at windows at night to

scare each other. The Co-Op started locking their grain bins, and I've patrolled the local fields a lot. The only place left is here."

"Or the farmers' market."

"I forgot about that." Bradley drops the cob into the pile and shakes his head. "I guess I'll go there next Saturday."

I laugh. His dedication to stopping pranks is adorable.

"So, what's got you needing a cowboy cop?" He tips his hat, making me blush.

"Samuel invited me to dinner."

"Are you going?" His eyes fill with concern.

I nod. "I didn't want to, but he asked."

"Ashley, you don't have to do what he says, or what any guy says." He touches my elbow gently.

I swallow at his soothing touch, so contrasting to Samuel grabbing me in the hallway. "I know," I whisper. "It should be fine."

"Then why did you text me the emoji?" He rubs his thumb across the bend of my arm slowly, making it tickle. I smile.

"He said it was more of a work dinner, and I panicked after that. I'm afraid he might tell me something secretive."

Bradley drops his hand to his hip. I stare at it as if I'm jealous it's no longer on my arm. "Something about what I suspect?"

"Maybe. Who knows with him? That's why I think I need to go."

Bradley shifts his weight. He looks at me a few seconds before responding. "I'm going with you."

I laugh nervously. On one hand, that would be awesome, if for no other reason than to see the look on Samuel's face. Instead, I say the other half of what I'm thinking. "Wouldn't we get more information if I'm alone?"

"True." He rubs his jaw and stares ahead at nothing in

particular. Then he turns to me. "You think it's time to wear a mic?"

"Excuse me." A young guy with a cart comes by and starts inspecting powdered donuts on the wall behind us.

Bradley nods toward the aisle, and we walk together slowly.

"And record what he says?" I ask in a low voice once we're out of earshot from the stock boy.

"Yes. And I could be nearby to hear it in case things get out of hand."

I suck in a deep breath and exhale. "You'd be close by?"

He takes a step closer to me and nods. One side of his mouth cocks into a confident grin. My heart skips a beat.

"That would be wonderful." My throat catches on the end of "wonderful." I said that a little too loudly and excitedly. Bradley's mouth morphs into a huge grin, embarrassing me further.

"All right. Let's stroll through the canned corn and plan a meeting time and place."

I continue beside him to the canned vegetables. "Wait, why would they want canned corn? That wouldn't make any noise."

He sighs. "You were never a teenage boy, but I was. They don't always think things through."

I laugh so hard I snort, causing Bradley to laugh too. I wish he could come to dinner at Samuel's. It would be way more entertaining.

CHAPTER THIRTEEN

Bradley

"Let's see." My hand shakes as I move closer to Ashley's shirt. "Why don't you run it up under there." I hand her the end of the microphone. She sticks it through the bottom of her shirt and clips the tiny end to the back of her pants. Then she positions the tail of her shirt over it.

"Can you put this in the best spot?" She holds up the end that will record.

"Yeah." I reach closer, uncomfortable at how close it lies to her chest. I knew I should've brought the longer cord. I was so worried about her being comfortable wearing it that I didn't account for me being comfortable helping her. The fact that we're parked down a dirt road at night doesn't help.

"Let's clip it right under your collar, pointing up. Unless he gets super close to your chest, he shouldn't notice it." I clear my throat. Mentioning her chest makes me feel like a middle-school boy.

She moves her hand toward her shirt opening, making things worse. "I could clip it to my bra."

"No!" I touch her wrist to stop her. "It will be fine at the edge of your collar." Before she digs in her shirt, making me even more unnerved, I take the mic and secure it to her shirt collar. "There." My fingers tingle as I slide them away.

"I knew it!" She stares at my hand.

"What?" My stomach pits. Did I accidentally offend her?

"I thought you were right-handed." She smiles.

"Well, yeah." I hold up my right hand. "About ninety percent of the world is."

She narrows her eyes. "Then why did you play against my dad with your left hand?"

I scratch my chin, amazed that she noticed. "Yeah, I did."

"Why?"

"I wanted to look competitive without demolishing him."

She smiles widely, making me smile. I'm a little embarrassed at admitting that. To save myself from further embarrassment, I don't dare mention that I won the Bubba Gump Southeast Regional Ping-Pong Tournament in Boy Scouts.

I palm the back of my neck and go back into sheriff mode to regain my confidence. "All you have to do is be yourself and act natural. I'll park nearby and monitor everything." I put my hand on her shoulder, which I feel is safe. "And if Samuel gets crazy or mean, I'll intervene."

She nods, then takes a deep breath and wrings her hands. I give her shoulder a squeeze. "You'll be fine." I release my hand before I'm tempted to pull her in for a hug. "I'll be down the street."

"Okay."

I step aside and shine my flashlight until Ashley is back in her car. Then I climb inside my truck and follow her to the main road. When she reaches Samuel's neighborhood, I hang back.

He lives in one of the bigger houses down the street from Morgan Archer. Half her yard is covered with kid stuff, and the other half has a county school bus, making it the perfect place to hide in plain sight. I pull on the other side of the bus and roll down my window. Samuel's house is lit up, and I can see inside most of the first level.

He answers the door and greets Ashley. His voice grinds through the radio like a squeaky wheel. I try to focus on what he says, which isn't much better. He goes on about what he's prepared for dinner. I roll my eyes when he mentions having a cheesecake shipped from New York that he's saved for a special occasion.

The next few minutes are filled with Ashley making baby talk to the pet rabbit, followed by Samuel bragging about a recent golf tournament. I lean against the door, halfway dozing off.

"What are we listening to?"

I jerk my head to Morgan standing beside my truck.

"I'm on a stakeout," I say.

"Nothing's wrong, is it?" She squints and makes a mean face. "Because this is my neighborhood, and I can help you throw down if needed."

"Trust me, Morgan, if I need an informant in this area, you'll be my first call."

She munches on a powdered donut, then wipes the dust from it down her pant leg. "Why are you in my yard and staring at Samuel's house? Is that who we're listening to?"

"I'm listening to Samuel, and it's none of your business."

She crosses her arms. "You're on my property."

I sigh. "Fair enough."

Morgan giggles and gets in the passenger side. "Who do you think is gonna win the Bama game this weekend?"

I shush her. She pouts and takes a bite of her donut. I lean closer to hear Samuel over her chewing.

"You know, being nosy like this might be part of the reason you're not married yet," she comments.

I stare at her.

"What? At least I've been married once."

I shake my head as she wipes donut dust on my seat. She notices me and pauses. "Oh, where are my manners? Would you like a donut?" She lifts the bag. It's identical to the ones the guy was pulling from the Pig earlier today.

"No thank you."

"Suit yourself." She shrugs. "I got them free from work. Can you believe they were gonna throw these out?"

I'm now mildly disturbed since I've eaten a lot of her food at potlucks before. Maybe she only goes for bad snacks and not ingredients.

"Who's he talking to?" she asks.

I shush her, then whisper, "Ashley."

"Bank Ashley?"

I nod.

"You like her, right?"

"I like a lot of people."

Morgan makes a mild hissing sound, which I take as disbelief.

"She's my campaign manager, and he doesn't want me to win. We think he's trying to sabotage my reelection."

There. So I lied. Or maybe I didn't. I wouldn't put it past Samuel to try and sabotage my campaign, and we may as well make the campaign thing official since it's spread all over two counties.

Samuel finally quits blabbing about golf and how he marinated the steaks. They sit in silence for a minute, but Morgan doesn't. She's snoring, and I'm a little jealous that she can go from wide awake and loud to dead asleep in a minute's time.

"I thought you needed to talk about work," Ashley says.

I turn up the volume.

"I do," Samuel says. "I wanted to thank you for all your hard work and let you know I plan on giving you more responsibility."

I lean in. This could be what we're wanting.

"More responsibility?" Ashley asks.

"Yeah, maybe a special project."

Here we go. I'm practically drooling over catching him confessing to corruption. Morgan's drooling too, on my leather seats.

More silence on the radio. I hear a bit of shuffling, then someone gasps. I straighten, ready to defend Ashley if needed.

"Samuel, I need to go."

"So soon? We haven't eaten the cheesecake yet."

"I know, but I—" Ashley groans. "I don't feel so well."

I stare out the windshield as she exits down his porch steps. Samuel stands at the door until she drives away. I don't move for fear he will hear or see my truck. And when Morgan snores even louder, I roll up the window.

After a few minutes, I call Ashley. "Everything okay?"

"Yeah, I was ready to get out of there. Sorry I didn't get more for you."

"No, it's okay."

"Can I give you back the mic tomorrow? I'm going to head home."

"Uh, yeah. Need me to follow you?"

"No," she answers quickly. "I'm fine now that I'm not in his house."

"Understandable," I say. "Text me when you get home so I know you're safe, please."

"I will." She hangs up.

The radio signal turns to static. I mute the volume and stare at Morgan. She does some random throat noise, then stops breathing for a moment. I'm half-panicked, thinking I may have to give her CPR to wake her up. I reach out to check her pulse, and she jumps when I barely touch her. Well, that answers my question.

"What, where am I?" She glances around, wiping drool from her cheek with the back of her hand.

"My truck, your yard."

She blinks. "Oh yeah. I need to make sure my kids all got a bath."

"Yeah, stakeout is over. I need to go home too." I clear my throat. "Morgan, I know you like to talk—"

She puts her hand on my arm and gives me a serious look. This time it's way more sympathetic than mean. "I won't mention this. I do like to gossip, but I also know how to keep my mouth shut when it matters." She half smirks. "That's the only way my kids don't think their daddy is pure scum."

I nod. "I appreciate that."

She pats my arm and climbs out of the truck.

Once she's in her house, I ease out of the drive and head home to wait on Ashley's text.

Ashley

I park near the trees to the side of Apple Cart Baptist Church. If I hadn't made plans with Carolina already, I wouldn't be here. Samuel will likely strut by any moment and make things awkward.

It's bad enough that I have to work with him tomorrow.

I gather my purse and Bible and maneuver through the gravel parking lot. I'm a little early for service, which means I'll need to wait around until Carolina and Jonah get out of Sunday school.

Soon as I climb the front steps, one of the doors swings open. Bradley stands on the other side, smiling.

My heart skips a beat for two reasons. First, I didn't expect him. Second, it's Bradley.

"Good morning, Miss Ashley. Fancy seeing you here."

Southern gentleman is a nice look on him. Especially since it includes perfectly combed hair and khaki-colored Wranglers.

"Good morning."

"It's good to have you." He opens the door wider for me to enter.

I notice a badge and walkie-talkie on his belt. "Are you patrolling here?"

He chuckles. "For the county, no. For the church, yes." He unclips his badge and holds it up for me to see. It reads, "Apple Cart Baptist Church Security Team."

"Nice." I smile as he clips it back.

"Can I direct you somewhere?" His eyebrows shoot up, highlighting his eyes.

"I'm waiting on someone to get out of Sunday school."

"Samuel?" The disgust in his voice is evident. "Sorry, that was rude."

I laugh. "Don't apologize. I'm meeting Carolina."

"Oh." His face relaxes. "She's upstairs in the couples' class."

"Do you go to a Sunday school class?" I ask.

Bradley stops a few feet from the elevator and lets out a

small laugh. "I always volunteer for security during this hour. It can be awkward if you're not a couple."

I twist my mouth, thinking about the few times I visited that Sunday school with Samuel. It was awkward for me because most people were either married or engaged. And with Samuel, I never felt like we were really together.

A big part of me believes Samuel wants a girlfriend to complete his image. Someone to take to events and show off to colleagues. He thinks it's expected of him to have a companion, but prefers to be alone.

"What about the singles' class?"

Bradley full-on laughs this time. "It's like a small-town meat market. I visited once two Sundays in a row, and seven women brought me casseroles the following week."

Now it's my turn to laugh. "That's a week's worth of food."

He shakes his head. "Not worth it."

We continue to the elevator, and he presses the button. I stare at the ceiling, waiting on the door to ding.

"It's good to see you're okay. I worried last night when you left suddenly." I lower my eyes to Bradley watching me. "I wanted to ask last night, but I respect your privacy."

I swallow. Funny how him respecting my privacy makes me want to share even more with him.

The elevator opens, and we step inside. When the door closes, my body temperature raises about ten degrees. I'm alone in a small enclosure with Bradley. Very similar to last night when he helped me with the wire. Which I need to return to him tomorrow.

I have no idea how he will react, but I have an overwhelming desire to be transparent about last night. Bradley leans against the back wall and smiles when I face him. I take a deep breath and exhale.

"Samuel kissed me last night!" I blurt out.

The elevator dings, and Bradley stretches across it to press the emergency button. It stops beeping, and a red light comes on. He doesn't look mad, but concerned—and a little hurt. It crushes my heart.

"Are you dating him again?"

I slump against the wall and shake my head.

"I'm sorry, it's none of my business." He wipes his hand over his head, then immediately smooths back his hair. I find it endearing.

"I'm just concerned, is all. Samuel's a bit of a wild card, and I never liked the way he talks to you when I'm around."

My heart speeds at him admitting concern. "I wanted to be transparent about why I rushed home. He kissed me, but I didn't kiss him back."

He plants his hands on his hips, then stares at the floor. After a long pause, he looks at me. "Did you want to kiss him?"

I shake my head. "I don't like him like that." I widen my eyes at the realization of what I'm about to say. "And a lot of days, I don't like him at all."

Bradley laughs. "I can understand that."

I pull my hair away from my face and push it behind my shoulder. Bradley drops his arms and takes a step toward me.

My heart thumps so fast, I expect it to beat through my dress. Like those old cartoons where it pounds in and out in a heart shape. I want to say that I like *him*, and that I like him like *that*.

But we're inside an elevator at church. Not exactly the time or place to do so.

"I'm glad you didn't kiss him back," he whispers.

"You are?" I hug my Bible to my chest as a reminder to stay focused.

He nods and grins. My insides melt. Starting with my brain, because what I say next is playing with fire.

"Why?"

He shrugs. "I'd like to think maybe you like someone else like that."

I tighten my arms around my Bible. *Focus, Ashley. What is wrong with you?* But my brain is hot wax dripping down to my heart. "Do you like someone like that?" I ask.

Yeah, I went there. I'm totally flirting now.

He shrugs again, then takes one step closer. My legs buckle, and I shift in my heels. "I do," he whispers even softer.

"Who?" I barely speak, meaning for it to stay in my mind. But the melted goo is seeping out even more. I need something to shut me up.

Oops. Wrong thought—or very right thought. As if reading my mind, Bradley presses his lips to mine.

The red light on the elevator blurs as I close my eyes and relax against the wall. His hand rests behind my head, and I enjoy the fantasy of kissing Bradley playing out IRL. Even better that it's in an elevator.

I've dreamed about making out with a hot guy in an empty elevator on several occasions. I just never assumed it would happen inside a two-story Baptist church.

Bradley pulls me closer to him, and I drop my purse and Bible on the floor. That's probably a clear sign we shouldn't be making out here, but I'm too far gone to reel it in now.

Unlike with Samuel, I can definitely say I kiss Bradley back. Then he kisses me back, then I kiss him back . . . then his walkie-talkie beeps.

"Bradley, this is Jack. I'm stuck in the fellowship hall making coffee. Can you check on the elevator for the senior adults?"

Bradley pulls away and jerks the device from his belt. "Ten-four," he answers.

His face and neck are flushed, and I imagine mine is the same. I run my fingers through my hair to untangle it.

"Well, that was fun while it lasted." He winks at me, and my legs buckle again. I hold on to the side to steady myself. He steps forward and unlocks the elevator, then turns to help me gather my belongings.

The door dings as I'm straightening my purse on my shoulder. A group of older people gives us haughty glares.

"About time you fixed it," Mrs. Maudy says. "We're going to miss our seats."

"My hip's out of whack from standing here five extra minutes," Ms. Ethel adds.

Bradley doesn't say a word. He simply nods and slides by them into the hallway. Paul pats him on the back as he passes. I follow and stare at the ground until the elevator door closes.

"Oh, here you go." Bradley hands me my Bible.

My eyes bulge when I notice crimson lipstick on the corner of his mouth. I'm sure I'm not the only one who noticed.

I take my thumb and rub it away. He smirks, catching on to what I'm doing. I drop my hand when voices come from down the hall. I hear Carolina's laughter and scoot away from Bradley. She's suspicious enough without any real evidence.

"Hey, there you are," she says.

Bradley and Jonah shake hands, and more people gather around us. We take the stairs to the main level for worship service. I hold tight to the railing, as my brain is still a bit foggy.

It's hard to process what happened, and it will be even harder to not think of it all afternoon while I'm shopping with Carolina.

CHAPTER FOURTEEN

Ashley

"Hey, Ashley."

I shift my gaze from the computer screen to Becki Douglas standing at my desk with a slim folder.

"Hi, Becki. Can I help you?"

"I wanted to drop off the questions for Thursday's debate."

She extends the folder, and I take it. A heaviness hits my stomach. When she'd mentioned getting questions to me, I expected a brief email with a few lines, not a folder that weighs more than my heaviest stack of bangle bracelets.

"This is so exciting. My first electoral debate." Becki grins and squeezes her hands in fists.

I paste on a fake smile until she turns around. Once she's out the door, I open the folder. The first page is labeled "Possible Questions." That gives me hope that she won't ask *every* question, but it also stresses me to think these are suggestions. What if she asks similar but not the same questions?

Good thing Bradley's good with words.

And that's not the only thing his mouth is good for. My neck heats up with the memory of our kiss.

I floated through the rest of the day in the best mood. Luckily, I love to shop so much that Carolina thought nothing unusual about my giddiness.

I force myself to focus on the present and flip through Becki's questions. She has them structured under categories. The last category is family.

This should have no bearing on whether a candidate would make the best sheriff. However, we're in Apple Cart County. There's a good chance a lot of the older population would favor someone with a family, even though I'm certain Bradley is settled.

A dangerous picture plays in the back of my brain. I'm snuggled next to Bradley on his couch, sipping coffee. A diamond ring is on my finger, and a couple of young kids run through the house laughing.

I slam the folder shut and take a deep breath. One kiss, and we're already married with kids in my mind. This is bad. So bad.

Even worse, I have no idea what that kiss means to him. It came after I asked who he liked, but was it an answer to that question or an impulse in the heat of the moment?

Either way, I need to set my personal feelings aside and do what I can to help him both win sheriff and get to the bottom of Samuel's weirdness. I pull out my phone and shoot him a text.

What are you doing for lunch?

· · ·

Three dots appear, then a response.

You tell me. ;)

A slight flutter hits my stomach. I press my hand to my rib cage, wishing a wink in a text didn't have that effect on me.

Can you meet at Mary's at noon?

Yep.

I fight the urge to send a cowboy emoji and drop my phone in my purse. For the next three hours, I'll bury myself in loan processing and paperwork. All the while trying to keep Bradley off my mind.

Every head turns when I open the door at Mary's. I really wish she'd take the bell off the top of the door, or at least grease the hinges. After everyone sees it's just me, they turn back around.

Except for one face framed by a tan cowboy hat. Bradley grins at me from across the room. I dip my head and warn myself to read nothing into it.

"Hello," he greets me. He tips his hat when I slide into the booth across from him.

To keep my emotions in check, I plop the folder on the

table and get right to business. "Becki brought this by the bank." I slide the folder toward him.

He takes it, brushing my fingers slightly. I coil my hand at the tingle it sends up my arm. I never anticipated it being this hard to work with him after kissing him.

Not that I anticipated kissing him . . . but I can't say I've been opposed to it all this time.

He opens the folder and clears his throat. A waitress stops by with two menus and some napkins. She looks vaguely familiar. "Hey, I'm Everly. Do you know what you want to drink?"

I order water, and Bradley gets sweet tea.

"Thanks. I'll be back with those in a bit."

An involuntary grin of satisfaction crosses my face when Bradley doesn't watch her walk away. She's super cute and friendly. I ignore the menu and focus on why I asked him to lunch. "That folder has possible questions for the debate on Thursday."

He skims through the pages. "So this is actually happening?"

I nod. "My biggest concern is the back page."

"Why?"

Everly arrives with our drinks. We thank her and order food.

"It's all about family," I say when Everly leaves.

Bradley lifts his face from examining the papers. "I have a family. Two parents, two older sisters."

I fold my hands and take a deep breath. "Hopper is married." I lift a hand before Bradley can respond. "Not that you should be, but a lot of older people will assume he's more settled."

"Settled? Like settled down?" Bradley crosses his arms.

"Yes, settled down here. You're ambitious, which is great,

but it makes you likely to marry a girl from somewhere else and move off."

"That's crazy." He huffs.

"I agree, but I know the people of this county."

"So I need to get married to a local girl?"

I laugh. "No. I'm simply saying we need to come up with solid answers to assure the people you're fully committed to staying in Apple Cart." I take a sip of my drink and watch Bradley thumb through the papers. "You are committed to staying here, right?"

He looks at me like I've grown an extra head. "Of course I am. This is my home."

I choose not to bring up that a few years back, he tried to woo back his ex who had moved to Atlanta. Talk around town was he offered to move if they got back together.

Everly brings our plates, and we thank her in unison. Bradley fixes his baked potato as he studies the questions. "I have nieces and nephews. We can mention that."

I shrug. "Do you do a lot with them?"

"No." He sighs. "They don't live here and are always busy with something."

I bite into my chicken sandwich and think of compelling evidence that Bradley is committed to Apple Cart for the long haul. "Could you buy the house you're in?"

"I could, but . . ." He trails off and starts cutting his steak.

"I'm sure Adrianne would sell."

"It's not that." He clears his throat and lowers his gaze. "I wanted to wait until I got married to buy a house and let my wife pick it out."

I almost choke on my water. This isn't good, considering I've had more than one daydream about being Bradley's wife.

He eats as if he didn't just throw a curveball at my brain. I cough and take a slow sip of my drink to gain control. Then

I focus on my food, hoping the conversation will shift naturally.

"Maybe you can pretend to date me."

I drop my sandwich on my plate. *Of all the ways for the conversation to shift!* My jaw hangs open as he stares at me coyly.

"If that makes you uncomfortable, we could always date for real." He winks.

A bolt of heat shoots through my body. Did he really say that? I attempt to reach for my food, but my hands won't move. I'm petrified.

He shakes his head. "I'm sorry. I didn't mean to make you uncomfortable."

"No," I protest. "I mean, you didn't make me uncomfortable." I'm lying through my teeth. The truth is he made me *very* uncomfortable. But in a good way. Like I'm uncomfortable because now I think he's on to me and how I feel about him.

Even though I hope there's another kiss, I can't possibly confess how much I want to date him. When—and if—we do date, I want it to be for no other reason than we both want to, not to impress old people.

We eat in silence a few minutes, which makes it even more awkward. I need to find a way to pivot this conversation. Right now I'm pinned against the proverbial wall like Ross Gellar.

"I may have a solution for getting you a companion."

"Oh really?" He smiles.

I feel myself blushing and dip my head. Picking at my side salad makes it easy to hide my face. "Yeah. I'll have to check on a few things first," I say without lifting my head.

"I see."

By the time I look at Bradley, he's busy polishing off his steak. My answer must've satisfied him, because he starts talking football and the weather. Or maybe he's uncomfortable now too, since those are go-to small-talk subjects in the South.

Regardless, my tension has eased by the time lunch ends. That is, until I realize I now have to come up with a solution to his companion issue.

Bradley

I've been down my share of dirt roads for both work and play. But I've never traveled down High Creek Drive in Sparrow, Alabama. It's at least as long as the driveway to Gamer's Paradise, with an even more narrow road. This reassures me I made the right decision in bringing my cop car.

The road ends at a large metal building with a huge chain-link fence to the side. This is the kind of place I expected Roy to find rattlesnake, not Ashley to find me a companion. But I'll play along for now.

Maybe it will make her jealous.

I park in front of the building and tuck my gun in my boot before getting out. A few dogs bark in the distance, and the wind whips an American flag on a pole nearby. When I reach the front porch, I see a metal sign on the building's front door engraved with "MAN'S BEST FRIEND." I hesitate, then knock on the door.

This is starting to look less like a potential rattlesnake refuge and more like a backwoods brothel.

The door opens to a pretty young woman with a long, dark braid. Her hair and eyes resemble my ex-girlfriend's, but

I'm certain I haven't met her before. I'd remember her for sure.

"Hi, you must be Bradley." She extends a hand.

I take it, and she gives me a firm shake. She drops my hand and swings the door wider. Ashley waves at me from the corner of the room. I lift my hand in greeting, then follow the woman inside. "And you are?"

She closes the door behind us and walks ahead of me. "Natalie." She keeps her head forward and doesn't speak again until she stops near Ashley.

I glance around the room, which is set up like an office waiting area. Natalie goes behind the counter, and I sit on a stool beside Ashley.

"Afternoon." I tip my hat to her.

She smiles. "Did you have trouble finding the place?"

I chuckle. "No, ma'am."

A loud plopping noise gets my attention. Natalie straightens a huge binder on the counter and opens it. "Ashley said you need a companion."

"Yeah . . ." I study Ashley for a hint of what's going on here.

She sips a coffee mug and settles back on her stool like it's commonplace to find people companions at a shop/office in the middle of nowhere.

Natalie clicks her tongue and flips through her binder. "Do you have a preference of size?"

Size? What does that even mean? And how do I answer that without sounding offensive?

"Uh, I don't care." My neck and ears itch when Natalie turns a page.

"Long hair or short?" She stares at me for an answer.

I admire Ashley's hair from the corner of my eye. "Long."

"Perfect." She flips another page. "Male or female?"

"Female!"

Natalie nods nonchalantly. "Good choice, they're easier to train."

I turn to Ashley for help. She's turned toward the wall, admiring a photo of a Dalmatian. Apparently, this kind of thing isn't odd in Moonshine County.

"I think I have the perfect fit for you, Bradley." Natalie slams the folder shut and grabs a key ring from the wall behind her. "Follow me."

Ashley hops off her stool and takes my hand. I blindly allow her to lead me behind Natalie through a door and down a long hallway. I close my eyes as Natalie unlocks a back room. Don't they know this is illegal? And for Pete's sake, I'm in uniform. Don't they care? This isn't Reno!

"Aww." Ashley's soothing voice forces my eyes open.

I exhale a huge sigh of relief.

Natalie motions us inside and shuts the door behind us. "Meet Trixie." She bends at the waist and pats her knees. The most beautiful long-haired German Shepherd trots toward her. A few other dogs notice us, then go back to chewing on their toys.

"Trixie is one of my rescues. I think she has the potential to one day work as a police K-9. She's smart, but gets a little distracted. Some time with a real cop might do her good."

I kneel and ruffle the dog's head. She pants happily.

"What do you think?" Ashley asks.

"A dog companion, huh?"

She shrugs. "Dogs make everyone more lovable, and she can be with you all the time."

I stand and smile at her. "Great idea."

Not as great as fake dating—or actually dating—her, but still better than what I thought was coming.

"So you're a K-9 trainer?" I ask Natalie.

She nods. "Yes. I've trained dogs most of my life, but moved to Alabama last year."

"Interesting."

"We met one day at Piggly Wiggly when she had a service dog with her," Ashley offers.

"Ashley asked to pet the dog, and I couldn't let her since it was in training to focus." Natalie laughs. "I could tell she felt bad for asking, so I explained."

"After that we became friends, and I come here sometimes to help out when she gets donations or new puppies."

"I didn't know that." I study Ashley's face. There's still so much I don't know about her that I want to discover. The fact that she loves dogs makes me like her even more.

"What do you think?" Ashley asks as she pets Trixie.

"I think I'll take both."

I clamp my mouth shut, embarrassed that I let that slip.

"Oh, Gretchen is going to a station in north Alabama next week," Natalie says.

I whip my head to see her petting a different dog that I assume is Gretchen. "That's cool. I didn't want Trixie to be lonely, is all." I try and play it cool.

Thanks to Natalie's swift response, Ashley might not catch the fact that I wanted to take *her* home with Trixie. But heck, they look downright adorable together.

"Trixie loves people," Natalie says. "Sometimes a little too much." She laughs. "That's one of the reasons we need to socialize her in different settings. So she can learn when to stay calm."

Ashley straightens and puts her hand on my arm. It gets that going-to-sleep tingling feeling. "And I can help with her too."

"I'd like that," I say. My voice is huskier and more of a whisper than I intended. Ashley stares at me and smiles. My heart pounds.

I've got a suspicion she's on to me.

CHAPTER FIFTEEN

Ashley

Bradley pulls up as I'm flipping the door sign to "Closed" at the bank. Trixie notices me from his cop car and wags her tail. I exit the bank and lock the door behind me.

Bradley meets me halfway to the car, and I wrap my hands around his forearms. This might be a little too forward, but I'm too excited. I've kept some big news to myself all day.

"We can take Trixie to the debate."

His forehead wrinkles, then he nods toward the car. "You can ride with us. I'll put her in the back."

He opens both doors on the passenger side, and whistles. Trixie bounds down from the front and hops in the back. He closes that door and wipes his hand across the front seat before I sit down. "Excuse the fur. She gets a little happy in the car and starts shedding."

"It's fine." I smile back at Trixie and buckle my seat belt.

She gives me a frustrated yelp from behind the prisoner partition. "You did nothing wrong, sweetie," I console her.

Bradley shakes his head at Trixie and laughs. "We have to work on her manners." He backs up and pulls onto the main road. "She'll be happy at the sheriff's office."

"That's what I've been trying to tell you. She can go with us now."

Bradley frowns. "I'm not taking a dog to Mary's."

I shake my head. "Becki called and said they're moving the debate."

"Where? Why?"

Before I can answer, we come to a standstill in front of Mary's. Several cars back out of the parking lot. A waitress comes out and tapes a handwritten sign on the door that reads, "Debate Moved to High School Stadium."

Bradley squints his eyes to read the sign, then stares at me, stunned.

"Becki thought we needed a bigger venue."

I watch his jaw muscles tighten as he swallows. He focuses ahead and crawls down the road behind the line of vehicles, all headed toward the school.

When we finally reach the school, Morgan jogs up to the car. She's wearing a bright orange vest and a whistle around her neck. I roll down my window to speak with her. She pants for a second and holds her side.

"Are you okay?" I ask.

"Yeah. That's the first time I've jogged in a while." She takes a deep breath, then continues. "Becki said to let you pass and park near the field."

She steps back and blows a whistle around her neck, then holds out a hand to the car behind us. She waves Bradley on and walks beside us until we're past the crowd and parked.

Trixie barks when Bradley opens her door. I meet them and take her by the leash.

"Oh good, there you are!" Becki rushes toward Bradley. She smiles at me, then gasps when she spots Trixie. "That dog is soooo adorable." Her voice creeps higher with every word.

"Thanks." I smile.

Becki pets Trixie, then grabs Bradley's sleeve. "We need you down on the field." She turns to me as she's pulling him away. "You can sit on the sidelines. There's a bench."

I follow them at a slower pace until I hear Mary's voice.

"Hey, sugar." I turn to the concession stand. She leans over the counter. "Need anything?"

"No, ma'am."

"I like your dog."

"Thanks, but it's Bradley's."

"Mm-hmm." She winks.

I face forward and keep walking. I hate it when she winks like she knows something nobody else knows.

Becki opens the gate to enter the field and closes it after we're all inside. She motions to an empty chair on one side of a podium. On the other side sits Vernon Hopper. Bradley stares at the field, then looks at me.

I grab his hand and give it a squeeze. "You've got this," I whisper.

He squeezes my hand back, sending a warmth up my arm. Then he releases me and takes his seat.

I lead Trixie to the bench on the sideline. She lies at my feet as I settle onto the metal seat. Becki stands behind the podium and smiles at the crowd.

Vernon flexes his arms, twice the size of Bradley's, which is saying a lot. To put it in perspective, if Bradley were Captain America, Vernon would be Thor.

Captain America . . . My mind wanders to Bradley dressed like him. That would sway this election in his favor.

He gives me a half smile after waving to the crowd when Becki introduces him. Trixie perks up when he looks our way. I let go of the leash to pet her head. But the second I touch her fur, she bolts toward Bradley.

And my idea of bringing her along for a newspaper photo op afterward slips away too.

Bradley

My heart pounds as Trixie barrels toward me like a bull out of the shoot. She hits my legs and plants her front paws on my knees, then licks my hand. I rustle her head as a collective "aww" hums through the stadium bleachers.

Great, now I'm even more nervous.

"Let's get to the questions." Becki smiles at the pup.

I take the leash to rein her in and relax a bit, knowing Becki isn't mad. Vernon gives me a snarl, and Ashley mouths "sorry" from the sidelines.

I shrug and smirk at her. Not much we can do to control a half-trained dog.

"We will begin by allowing both candidates a minute to introduce themselves." Becki fumbles with her phone. "Since not as many are familiar with Vernon, he can go first on this round."

She taps her phone screen, and Vernon stands. He talks about his wife and new baby more than anything, playing up the family angle. Smart guy—that's the ultimate way to one-up me. Well, besides maxing out on arm reps.

It's not warm tonight at all, but he decided to wear short sleeves rolled tightly over his biceps. I cross my arms and hope the women voters aren't shallow enough to let that entice them. I'm not used to being the older, less-fit guy in the running for something. But as long as nobody publicly blesses my heart, I may manage to keep some dignity tonight.

"And not that he needs much of an introduction here, but Sheriff Bradley Manning." Becki smiles at me.

I stand as the crowd claps, making sure to not drop Trixie's leash. She stands with me, panting. "I'm Bradley Manning, your current county sheriff. I'd be honored to continue carrying out all the progress we've made so far during my first term if you reelect me."

Trixie nudges my leg and whimpers. I pat her head, then swallow. "I don't have a beautiful wife and child." I pause and make eye contact with Ashley. "Yet." My neck burns, so I focus on the crowd again. "But I'd like to introduce y'all to Miss Trixie."

Trixie yelps when I say her name, getting a fond reaction from the stands. "With any luck, she will be part of the department one day and help our efforts to make Apple Cart County drug free. That is, if you trust me with a second term."

I tip my hat, smile, and sit. That's all I've got and the best I can do. Vernon can throw in his wife and kid all he wants. I have a record to stand on.

Trixie paws my leg, reminding me she's there. I rub her ears. Maybe she will bring me luck.

Becki asks several questions about our experience in law enforcement, which gives me a leg up. Vernon is younger and doesn't have a degree in criminal justice. Oh, and he doesn't have any sheriff experience.

I sit a little straighter, satisfied that my answers included way more credentials and examples of relatable experience.

Becki asks a few more specific questions, some submitted to her ahead of time by people in the community. It's not hard to tell which questions were hers and which belong to all of Apple Cart County.

We answer questions about the dilapidated water tower downtown, the pothole left from where they dug up the old railroad tracks, and the usual request for a local lottery.

I do my best to answer these without offending anyone. Nothing divides the residents of Apple Cart more than the original water tower. It's out of operation and a hazardous eyesore to some. To others, it's a local relic that should be deemed a historical landmark.

As for the pothole, it's been repaved twice in the past decade. If teen drivers would obey the speed limit on that side road, it wouldn't reappear so often.

Of course, I'm not so forward with my public response to those questions.

Becki's questions are much more practical. She asks about the crime rate, plans for the police force, and the concerns that Apple Cart County needs an official fire station.

I address each of those with confidence, ending with a nod to my love for this place. "I'm fully dedicated to protecting Apple Cart County and all its residents." I focus on Ashley. "And I don't plan on going anywhere. In fact, I've been on a covert mission to ensure this county remains the safe and secure place we all love."

Everyone in the bleachers applauds, and I tip my hat once more. My heart swells when I glance across the crowd at all the people I love so much. Vernon can't possibly care as much about this community as I do.

I glance at Ashley before I take my seat. She gives me a nervous grin. I come down a few notches from my moment of glory. If she looks nervous, should I be too?

A thousand reasons for her clenched smile run through my mind as Becki wraps up the debate. One conclusion is I took it a little too far when I stared at her and said, "I don't plan on going anywhere." I meant that about her as much as the town. And by her face, I'm guessing she knows that.

I'll have to learn to dial back my emotions and let her set the pace, even if she decides to kill the transmission on this steamroller she's driving over my heart.

CHAPTER SIXTEEN

Ashley

I exhale and take a big sip of my Stanley. This morning has been a whirlwind. It's Friday, and half the town has come by with paychecks to deposit and cash.

Despite our efforts to offer direct deposit, many of the town businesses still cut checks, and many of the older generation insist on getting paper checks because they don't trust the internet.

On days like this, I jump behind the extra teller window and get to work. It's usually a welcome pace from sitting behind my desk and processing loans.

Today is different. I got maybe two hours of sleep last night and haven't managed to eat anything today. Everything that happened at the debate has my head spinning.

Bradley mentioned a covert mission, and I'm scared to death Samuel is on to us.

When the debate ended and half the town was greeting

Bradley, I kept an eye out for Samuel. He never came near us, but he did show up in my dreams. The little sleep I did get was plagued with a nightmare in which he took over the mic at the debate and called out Bradley and me for spying on him.

Add to that the fact that Bradley was uncharacteristically quiet on the ride back to my car, and I have a scary suspicion he might be nervous too.

This whole cover-up is getting to my head.

I drain the remaining water from my Stanley and almost choke as Samuel's voice rings in my ear. "Ashley."

I cover my mouth and cough. Then I jump when I turn to him right behind me. "You scared me," I whisper.

His lips curve coyly, reminding me of the Grinch. A chill runs down my spine. He must be on to us.

"Now that the rush is dying down, I could use your help in the back."

Think, Ashley.

I glance at the clock on the wall. It's one-twenty. "Could I go to lunch first?"

He frowns, but nods. "I suppose we can manage the rush."

Where was he an hour earlier? The lobby is now empty except for Paul counting suckers by the kiosk.

Instead of pointing out the obvious, I seize the moment and hurry to my desk. I gather my purse and rush toward the door. The sound of suckers bouncing onto the tile dings behind me, but I don't dare stop. Samuel would want me to straighten Paul's mess, then offer to order me takeout. I have to leave now or I'll be here all day.

I burst through the glass door and blink at the sun like a prisoner going out for recess. Thankfully, I have a car that allows me to leave the prison grounds for an hour.

I text with one hand as I back out of the parking lot. One

simple emoji.

Three dots blink. But I'm on the road and on the clock. I panic and call him.

"Ashley?" Bradley's voice on the other end has an immediate calming effect on me.

"Hey." My voice is breathy.

"What's wrong?"

I squeeze my stomach to fight the mixture of hunger and nerves. "Samuel asked me to help him in the back, and I panicked."

"Where are you now?"

"At the red light."

That would sound ambiguous anywhere but Apple Cart. We have one actual traffic light.

"Come by Big Butts. I'm here."

I turn down a side road, thankful he's at a restaurant. Technically a permanently parked food truck, but one with great barbecue.

I arrive to Bradley propped against the front of the truck, his sunglasses reflecting the afternoon sun. He pushes off the trailer and walks toward me when I park.

He greets me with, "You okay?" when I open my door.

I waver my head.

"How did you leave?"

"Lunch break."

"It's close to two."

My stomach rumbles at the news. I put a hand on it and stare at the ground.

"Come on." Bradley takes my hand and leads me to the trailer window.

Billy Bob turns from washing some pans and comes to the opening. "Hey, what can I get y'all?"

Bradley smiles at me and nods toward the menu.

"I'll have a pulled-pork salad and some water."

"Add a sweet tea and some curly fries," Bradley says.

"All right."

Bradley drops my hand and pays for the food. A young girl helping inside pushes our drinks onto the windowsill, and our food is out in a few minutes.

Juggling the to-go boxes and his tea, Bradley manages a free hand to hold mine. His touch is protective and calming all at once. We pass my car and walk toward the tree line, where his cop car is parked. He drops my hand once more to open the passenger door.

Once inside the car, we can talk freely.

"Now you have food, and we're literally off the beaten path." He smirks at the gravel-and-dirt side road behind Big Butts, then turns to me. "A little cop secret: stake out near a restaurant for easy provisions."

I laugh, allowing a bit of tension to release. He opens our food and hands me both boxes.

"These are yours," I say, holding the fries.

"Nope. I ate an hour ago. I got these for you."

I raise a brow.

"I have two sisters and a mom. I can tell when a woman needs carbs."

I brush a strand of hair behind my ear and dip my head. He no doubt heard my stomach growl.

"Go ahead, enjoy. You've got the best figure in all of central Alabama." He removes his glasses and scans me, then meets my eyes. "Trust me, I've attended a few county pageants."

I laugh, imagining Bradley judging the Apple Sauce Queen Pageant at the county fair. Then I dip a fry into my cup of ranch dressing and pop it in my mouth. He was right. I did need carbs.

Bradley sips his tea and leans back in his seat while I eat. This is in no way a date, but I like to think that it could be.

Between Samuel and the reelection drama, neither of us has addressed anything about *us*, including the hot elevator kiss.

"What's your plan when you go back to work?"

I sigh.

"Do you need me to pop in the bank?"

I shake my head and drink some water.

"I don't want you in the back room with him if you're scared." He takes my hand for the third time.

But this time is different. He has the same look in his eyes as he did before we kissed. My chest rises and falls, and I take a deep breath.

Is he about to kiss me? In a cop car?

First a Baptist church elevator and now a cop car. Bradley has a way of bringing romance to the most unexpected places.

His eyes trail toward my lips, then meet my eyes again. "Uh, would it be okay if I wired you?"

"What?" I blink. My mind was fixed on a kiss, but maybe his wasn't.

"I know you don't like being close to him, so I can listen live in case you need me to rescue you."

Rescue you. Most women I know would pitch a fit at that comment and declare their self-reliance. However, I read deeper into what those words mean coming from Bradley.

He wants to keep me safe and comfortable. To not put me in a situation where I would need to protect myself. No other man, short of my dad and grandpa, has cared so much for my safety.

"Sounds like a plan." I half smile.

He nods. "Give me a minute."

He gets out of the car and rummages in the trunk. I exhale and check my teeth in the mirror for any stray strands of lettuce or pork. If he does decide to kiss me, I wouldn't want my smile to change his mind.

"Okay." Bradley returns with the same device we used before.

I take it from him and untuck my blouse, then run the wire like last time. Then I hand him the mic end. He adjusts it beneath a button on my blouse. My chest heats up when his fingers graze my collarbone. His hand shakes slightly, letting me know it affects him as much as it does me. I swallow and keep my calm while he hides it behind the neckline.

"There." His mouth twitches in a half-nervous, half-playful way that I find endearing.

"Where do I put this?" I stare at my pencil skirt. I don't have a pocket or stiff jeans to clip the end.

He twists his mouth and studies my skirt. "Turn around."

I twist in the seat so he's facing my back. He takes the tiny box dangling from the cord and gently lifts the end of my blouse. My chest grows hotter when his fingertips graze the top of my skirt. He stops at the button and zipper in the back. "Uh, I think if you clip it behind the zipper part and turn it upward, we can hide it under your shirt."

"Okay," I whisper.

"If you'd rather . . ."

"I trust you," I whisper.

He gently clips it to the back of my skirt, barely touching my lower back with his fingertips. Then he lifts my blouse and tucks it in gently, tickling my skin.

He's so careful to keep his hands high and light that it makes me like him that much more. Samuel, and most other guys I know, would take advantage of a woman in this position and make a sport out of pinning the wire on the girl's lower back.

His hand moves, and my skin chills at the lack of touch. "There. You probably want to make sure your shirt looks good in the back."

I turn in the seat, careful to not bump the wire. Bradley lifts the tiny earpiece I wore before. "And this."

I take it, slowly grazing my fingers against his. I situate it in my right ear.

"You can see it some. May I?"

I nod. He leans closer and brushes my hair over my shoulder. Then he moves it slightly. "Does that feel good?"

His fingers brushing my hair away from my neck? Heck yeah!

"It's good," I say.

He moves back, but keeps his hand on my neck. Our eyes lock, and I place my hand on his in an effort to grant him permission to kiss me.

He leans forward again, and I close my eyes. We're close enough for me to feel his breath against my cheek when radio static bursts beside us. "Suspicious activity on the west side of town. Possibly hazardous materials and illegal activity."

Bradley groans and I open my eyes to him grabbing his radio. "Ten-four. Headed that way."

"I should probably get back anyway," I say when he lowers the radio. "Thanks for lunch."

He nods and smiles sadly. Then he backs up and drives me to my car. I get out and start to clean up my lunch remains.

"I'll get it later. You be safe." He stares at me, then puts on his sunglasses when I close the door.

I watch him peel out of the Big Butts parking lot with his siren blaring, then get in my car. All the while hoping he won't need to burst in the bank with sirens once I help Samuel.

"Ashley."

I've no more than dropped my purse under my desk when Samuel calls my name from the hallway. I grit my teeth, halfway wishing I hadn't come back.

I straighten and turn toward his voice. He's propped against the wall, smug look on his face. Little does he know I have a lifeline threaded under my blouse. The mic rests against my collarbone, giving me a hint of assurance that I can withstand whatever is waiting in the back room.

Samuel opens the back room door and waves me inside, then shuts it behind us. I blink to adjust my eyes to the florescent lighting. It's like entering a time warp compared to the recessed lighting and modern fixtures up front.

"I need you to hold off on the usual boxes and copy something else first." He pulls out a smaller box hidden in the corner of the room and sets it by the copier. The papers inside look somewhat newer than the others. I assume this is something he made more recently.

The top page is for Piggly Wiggly. Until now, all the papers I've copied had the names of individuals. If he's transitioning to naming businesses, this is a whole new level of slimy.

"I need these done today so we can mail them. Only one copy this time, so it shouldn't take that long."

I nod, my stomach churning. Something about this box seems even seedier than before. Knowing Samuel like I do, I play to his weakness for organization. "Should I stuff them in envelopes or stack them any certain way?"

"Separate envelopes for each company would be great. Those big manila ones you girls keep for large cash withdrawals."

"I can run and get some," I offer. I try not to smile too much with the satisfaction that my plan worked.

"Hurry back, and I can show you how to organize them."

I rush toward the front and grab a stack of envelopes from the cabinets behind the teller station. Then I throw on the sweater I keep draped over my desk chair and slip my phone in the pocket.

Back inside the room, I set aside the envelopes, then shove my hands in my pockets and shiver. "I knew I couldn't stay near that vent long without a cardigan."

He nods. I keep my hands in my pockets, playing into the shivering effect. What he doesn't see is that I hit the Record button on my phone. I positioned it so the camera is poking above my pocket, facing outward. It might not be the best footage, but it should do in case I need to hold up a document for evidence of the originals.

I take the top sheet and line it up on the copier. After hitting the Print button, I turn to Samuel behind me. I arch a brow, questioning his looming presence. Is he on to me making extra copies?

My pulse races as he steps closer and lays his hand on mine. I throw up a little in my mouth when our eyes meet. "I know things have been different between us lately." He rubs his hand over mine.

I shift uncomfortably. I swear if he tries to kiss me, I'll dump the box of papers on his head and call Bradley.

"Nothing wrong with keeping things professional," I say, emotionless.

"I didn't want you to think I was making you do menial work. This is *very* important."

I slide my hand out from under his to retrieve the paper and set a new one inside the copier. "I'm good. You can go back to whatever you were doing before."

He nods and exits the room slowly. Not until the door is closed and I see that he's gone do I relax.

With every paper I copy, I add the step of holding it so my phone can see the name of the company before I lay it flat on the copier. About two-thirds through the box, my earpiece buzzes.

"Everything all right?" Bradley asks.

"Yep."

"If you need anything, use the code word 'cowboy.'"

I giggle.

"What's so funny?"

I turn to Samuel in the doorway. I swear he's now a ninja. "Oh, not much." I hold up a paper. "The name Big Butts always makes me laugh."

He frowns. "You don't have to read them."

"I thought you wanted them in separate envelopes?" I challenge. Knowing I have Bradley in my ear gives me an added level of confidence.

"True." He twists his wrist and stares at his watch. "It's getting late. Why don't you go on home."

"Do you need me to take these and mail them for you?" I thumb the stack of envelopes with the papers inside.

"No," he answers a little too eagerly. "I have to address them properly and add some more details."

I lift my chin and wait for him to continue or excuse me for good. It takes a minute, but he gets the hint.

"Here." I hand the paper I'm holding to Samuel, careful to tilt it in the direction of my phone as I do.

He steps closer to me and takes it. His hand lingers a second, and I drop mine. I can't tell if he's testing me or trying to flirt. Either way, it's not worth me hanging around to find out. I gather my purse and leave as quickly as I did for lunch. Except this time instead of calling Bradley, I talk to him through the wire. "I'm leaving."

"Hey, if you're not in a hurry, swing by the sheriff's office and bring the wire."

I turn the video off my phone and grin. "I've got something even better. See you in a minute."

CHAPTER SEVENTEEN

Bradley

I stand inside the open garage door and wave Ashley's tiny black car inside. Once she's parked, I immediately close the door like Batman has entered the Bat Cave.

"In case that worm drives this way, he won't spot your car." I wink.

Ashley blushes lightly, and I love that I have that effect on her. I open the back door to the sheriff's office and motion her inside. My personal office is a few doors down, which means we don't have to pass anyone.

Not that I have anything to hide, but I'm well aware of everyone's interest in spotting Ashley with me. There's only so long we can blame it on the campaign. With any luck, by election day, we can come clean.

My plan is to have Samuel behind bars or, at the least, out on bail by then. And if Ashley decides to openly profess her love for me, that would be icing on the cake.

I glance her way to gauge her demeanor. Her lips curve slightly, a sense of calm over her face. Much more relaxed than earlier today when she drove up to Big Butts.

She untucks her shirt and fumbles with the back of her skirt. *What the . . .*

I momentarily forgot she's wearing the wire until she unhooks the mic and fishes it out of her shirt. She hands it to me, and I'm jealous of its warmth. No fair that it got to spend hours hugging her neck and back.

"And the something extra." She hands me her phone.

"What's on this?"

She shrugs. "I've yet to see, but I had it on record and tried to strategically keep it in my pocket." She sticks her hand back inside the sweater pocket and holds it up.

"Good thinking." I'd debated using a camera wire before but decided against it, knowing the camera would be with the mic. I wouldn't dare think of asking Ashley to hook a camera to her chest area. That seems inappropriate on too many levels. Not to mention how mad it would make me if it got a close-up of Samuel.

Hearing about a kiss between them is bad enough. Seeing one might drive me to barge in and handcuff him.

The fact that it bothers me so much says I care a lot about her. Only one other woman has made me jealous, and those feelings have long faded. Heck, I even share interesting work stories over sweet tea with her doctor husband when they're in town.

I sit in my office chair and stare at her phone. "Could you help with this?" I lift it.

"Oh yeah." Ashley laughs.

She looks at her screen to unlock it. Then she scrolls to the photos and hits a video. I press Play and hide a smile when she sits in the chair beside mine. I'm used to that seat being occupied by coworkers and people spouting out problems. Not a pretty woman I'd want to take on a date.

She's here on assignment, I remind the runaway train in my brain that's headed for the clouds. I focus my attention to the phone.

Random views of the copier and the wall take up most of the footage. Samuel's voice can be heard in the background, and at one point, there's a terribly close-up view of his slacks. Even though it's his knees and not his face, I know with a shot like that, he has to be within inches of her. I grit my teeth when he says something about not making her do menial work. More like making her do dirty work. Stupid snob.

A sick feeling pings my gut. I'm not a rich banker with showy hair and gold jewelry. But I am using her to spy. Guilt grows inside me while we watch the remainder of the video. I try and make note of the local businesses on the documents, but the rest of my mind is caught up in crafting an apology.

The video ends, and I slide the phone on my desk. I run a hand down my face and exhale deeply.

"Is it that bad?" Ashley's eyes widen.

"What?" She catches me off guard.

"What he put on the documents?"

"Oh, I'm not sure. We can get screenshots for more details."

"I should've made an extra copy, but he was standing there half the time."

"Hey, you did good." I touch her arm.

Her big doe eyes stare at me with uncertainty, and I can't keep it in any longer. "Ashley, I feel awful making you do this."

"You didn't make me." She pats my hand that's still resting on her forearm.

"I'm not talking about the phone." I glance at it, then

back at her. "All this. You having to be in uncomfortable situations with Samuel and spy on him."

She sighs and shakes her head. "I can handle Samuel."

A small chuckle hangs in my throat. "I never thought you couldn't, but I'd hate for things to go badly if he suspected you."

"Nobody wants to see if Samuel's doing something sleazy more than me, trust me." She half smiles and squeezes my hand. "And if there's anyone I would want to work with on that, it's you."

My mouth turns from a pitying droop to a smile. "I want to make sure you're safe and comfortable with everything. That's all. If anything ever gets to be too much in any way—"

Ashley plants a quick kiss on my lips before I can finish my sentence. Then we lock eyes, and I'm too caught up in the deep blue outlining her pupils to finish my train of thought. If that's not bad enough to cause a train wreck in my head, she leans against my neck and whispers in my ear, "You have always made me feel safe and comfortable."

I dip my head and find her lips. Brushing her hair out of her face, I tilt to kiss her. She kisses me back and wraps her arms around my neck. We fall in deeper, and I curl my fingers in her hair. It's almost as hot as the elevator kiss until I hear a beep.

I ignore it at first, knowing there are other people in the building. It beeps again, and I try and forget all responsibility, but can't remember if we shut the door.

I kiss her harder, then hear the smoke alarm in the hallway. Okay, I can't ignore that. I am the law, after all. Reluctantly, I pull back and drop my hands from cradling her head. She smiles at me sweetly, her lips full from our kiss. I rub my thumb across her cheek as I stand and twist my chair away from her.

"Sorry, I better check on that," I say on my way to the

door, which is closed. I enter the hall to a burning smell and speed up. The only person I see in this end of the building is the overnight desk clerk. And she's watching *The Office* on her computer screen.

"Cassidy!" I hurry toward her and spot earbuds hanging behind her pink hair. Not wanting to scare her, I rush to the front of her desk and wave my arms. She notices me after a few seconds and pokes out her bottom lip as if disturbed. "Cassidy!"

She plucks out an earbud and meets me on the other side of the window. "Yes sir?"

"Do you smell smoke or hear a beep?"

She wrinkles her nose, and mine instantaneously itches at the hoop ring dangling from it. She sniffs the air, then her eyes grow wide as saucers. She jumps, sending her rolling chair into the wall.

I follow her on a sprint toward the kitchen. The beep is the oven, and so is the smoke. She opens the oven door to what appears to have once been a pizza. It's now a charcoal circle.

I grab the fire extinguisher from the closet nearby and spray the crap out of it. The smoke sizzles as the pizza turns to foam.

Cassidy blinks and gives me a dumbfounded stare.

"Is this your pizza?" I motion toward the oven.

"It was," she pouts.

"Could you not smell the smoke?"

"Nah. My nose piercing hit a nerve, and I ain't smelled much since."

I palm my face. "You need to keep your earbuds out so you can hear. What if someone called?"

"The phone lights up."

I cross my arms.

"Everything okay?" We both turn to Ashley in the doorway.

"It is now." I shake my head at the oven.

She grits her teeth. "Are you okay?" she asks Cassidy.

Cassidy scrunches her face, hiding her thin eyebrows under her pink bangs. Then she turns to me.

"You're not fired . . . yet."

She exhales. Ashley blinks, obviously confused at what happened.

"I promise I won't cook pizza with my earbuds in again," Cassidy pleads. "I can't go back to working at DG."

"How about no earbuds while you work?" I counter with my hands firmly on my hips.

"One earbud?"

I pinch the bridge of my nose. "Fine, but if I hadn't been here, you'd be in trouble. Most of the volunteer firefighters live in Wisteria."

"Was she here?" She points to Ashley.

"I'm helping with his campaign," Ashley spouts out quickly, blushing a little.

"May I suggest we get a real fire department, then?" Cassidy asks her, then turns to me.

"Becki mentioned that, too, in the debate." I smirk. "Help me get reelected and I'll see what we can do."

Ashley

"Good morning!" I glance up from my desk to Aniston singing out a greeting.

"I'm putting out flyers around town and wanted to check if I could put one on the bank door."

I take the piece of paper she's holding toward me. It's an announcement about Jim Vann, the weatherman, holding a tornado demonstration on the baseball field.

"It's free, but the PTSO is selling concessions and tornado T-shirts as a fundraiser for the school."

"Tornado T-shirts?"

Aniston laughs. "Something Georgia came up with. Pretty much T-shirts torn up like they've been through a tornado."

"And people will buy those?" I raise a brow skeptically.

"With Jim Vann's signature, they will."

"True." I shake my head. The celebrity-crazed crowd around here idolizes the local weatherman. It only got worse when Coach Saban retired and the number-one radio show disbanded. They now focus all their attention on Jim Vann.

"I'll have to—" I stop myself. I'm sick of asking Samuel permission for every little thing. "I'll get you some tape."

"Thanks, girl." Aniston smiles.

I retrieve some tape from my desk drawer and hand it to her. If Samuel doesn't like it, he'll pull it down like he did Bradley's sign.

While Aniston hangs the flyer, I check my email. I stop scrolling when I see "Bama State Bank Job Opening" in the subject line. I met the branch loan officer at a conference last year, and I alluded to interest in working there one day. It's in Birmingham and has a lot of big business clients. At the time, Samuel and I hadn't quit officially going out.

And I hadn't gotten to know Bradley.

"Here's your tape back." I jump at Aniston's voice in front of me.

"Thanks," I muster. My neck itches like she's caught me doing something illegal.

Is it wrong to read an email about another bank job while I'm working my current bank job? I sigh and watch Aniston leave before opening the email. Maybe I'm extra edgy due to all the mess with Samuel's back-room copies and lying to the town about why I'm always meeting with Bradley.

It's not like we never discuss his run for sheriff. We just prefer to squeeze it in briefly between watching bank spy footage and making out.

I scan the email, my pulse picking up with every word I read. The loan officer is planning to retire soon, and they will post her job. She wanted to give me a heads-up to prepare my resume and use her as a reference in case I'm interested.

I hit Reply, then stare at the screen. No doubt, I'm interested. Working for a huge bank, living in a big city. That sounds like a dream.

Or it did a year ago.

Now I have a lot of friends and Bradley. Or I think I kind of have Bradley. Or maybe I could have Bradley.

I sigh and save the email so I can come back to it tonight. Homer Giles marches in, whistling. He tugs at his jeans, which sit below his belly. I close my personal email browser and open my work messages.

His heavy footsteps grow louder against the tile floor until they stop in front of my desk. I glance up, his belly square with my eyes. I wrinkle my nose. He usually goes straight to the teller window to cash his paycheck.

"Can I help you, Homer?"

"Yeah." He tugs at the back of his jeans, causing the front of his shirt to come untucked. "I need a loan."

"Oh. Have a seat." I nod at the chair in front of my desk.

He plops down, causing the chair legs to screech on the floor.

"While I pull up your account info, can you give me some details about the loan?"

"Yep. I need a business loan."

"Oh." As long as I've known Homer, he has worked on JoJo's logging crew. It will be interesting to see what kind of business he wants to start.

"I'm opening a liquor store."

"Where?" I raise my eyes from the computer screen.

He's kicked back with his hands folded behind his head, which unfortunately raises his shirt again. I glance away.

"I'm hoping to buy that empty lot near the park."

I sigh. "Homer, you do know Apple Cart is a dry county, right?"

"I'm hoping that's gonna change soon."

I shake my head. "I wouldn't hold your breath."

"I think Vernon would allow it."

"What's Vernon have to do with a wet or dry county?"

Homer drops his arms and leans forward. "When he becomes sheriff."

My chest rises with a primal instinct to defend Bradley. The sensible Southern belle inside me backs it down, and I take a deep breath to compose myself before answering. "The election hasn't happened yet, so we don't know who will win."

Homer laughs. I watch him straight-faced, waiting for him to stop.

"I know you can't say anything, helping out Bradley and all."

I suck in an even deeper breath.

"That's nice of you," he adds.

"Tell you what, Homer. Let the election pass, and we can see if the county goes wet or dry. If it goes wet, which would involve other votes besides the sheriff, or if you have any business ideas that don't involve alcohol, come back and see me."

He nods and smiles. Then he stands, screeching the chair across the floor once more.

I watch him march toward the door and grab a sucker on his way out. An older lady stands on the other side, and Homer holds it open for her.

"Thank you, son."

"You're welcome." He smiles. "Vote for Vernon, and I'll open us a liquor store."

The woman gives him a forced smile, then turns her head and shakes it. I drop my head on the desk.

Maybe moving to Birmingham isn't such a bad idea.

CHAPTER EIGHTEEN

Bradley

"I see, mm-hmm, yeah. Thanks, big dog." I hang up the phone and shake my head.

Someone called anonymously to tip me off about an illegal drug trade. If it's the senior-citizen women swapping prescription pills again, I'm going to lose it.

The only info I have is the buyer and seller are meeting at the end of a dirt road in Wisteria at six p.m. At least they had the name of the road. Checking out every dirt road in Wisteria would take a month of Sundays and then some.

I want to call and check on Ashley, but then she'll ask what I'm doing. Nobody needs to know about the drug trade, and she might worry even more if I don't specify why I'm working late. I just hope she's not having to stay late with Samuel.

Even thinking about him makes my skin crawl.

I close my door and grab a pair of dumbbells I keep in

the office closet. Pumping out a few dozen bicep curls always gets my adrenaline going. When you're a small-town sheriff, you never know who you're facing until you arrive at the scene. It could be a dangerous drughead, a group of old ladies, or even a wild animal.

I've gotten so many calls about animals over the years that I debated starting an exterminating service on the side.

Eleven, twelve . . . I mentally count the final few reps of the last set, then return my weights to the closet. It's time to close down my office and hit the road.

I say goodbye to some of the weekend staff as I head out the door and journey toward Wisteria.

The one red light stops me near the bank. I don't see Ashley's car or anyone else's. Instead, a campaign sign for Vernon flaps in the wind. His muscled-up chest twists back and forth like he's taunting me to fight. If I weren't trying to act mature and didn't have other cars behind me, I'd jump out, beat his plastic face in, then go about my night.

Instead, I refrain and aim to beat him in the election.

I drive through Apple Cart and Wisteria to the more secluded part of the county. Most of the roads are now dirt, and I slow down to not miss the one where the deal is going down. It's technically a log road and doesn't have a name. But I know it well since I caught a group of high schoolers trespassing on it not long ago. They pretty much gave themselves away by shooting fireworks in August.

I ease down the road with my lights dimmed to not draw attention. It's a few minutes after six, which means any prompt drug dealers should already be conducting business.

My plan is to sneak up on them in the act.

I park a few feet back from the clearing behind a log loader. Then I clip my gun to my side and get out. Voices carry from the other side of the clearing.

Thank God nobody is here to witness my sneaking walk,

which Kyle says looks like a bad impression of army snipers moving on a video game. But if I catch these dealers, who cares.

My eyes bug when I see Samuel. It takes all my willpower not to scream with joy. He's caught red-handed, and as an added bonus, this means he's not with Ashley tonight.

I squat behind a pile of sawdust and listen. I somewhat recognize the other voice, but his back is to me.

Heavyset rednecks are a dime a dozen around here, so I don't want to profile the guy too soon. However, there's no mistaking the guy with the slick hair and suit is Samuel. I inch closer and listen as he mentions Vernon.

Now it's getting interesting.

The most interesting part is nothing is exchanged. No money or bags or even a handshake. Just words.

Then Samuel steps into the shadows, and I hear his car crank. When it sounds distant, the guy turns around and spits a wad of tobacco. On. My. Shoulder.

I wince and toss a handful of sawdust on top to try and soak it off my uniform. Aggravated, I stand and face him. "Homer Giles, you are under arrest."

"For what?" His face pales.

"Spitting on an officer."

He balks. "How was I to know you was there, Bradley? Nobody's supposed to be here."

"Well I am, and I heard your conversation with Samuel."

"You ain't supposed to be here. This is somebody's land."

"Then why are you here?"

"JoJo's got us logging it."

I cross my arms, causing some of the sawdust to flake off. "Well I work the whole county, and this land is in my jurisdiction. I heard you mention Vernon and drugs. Care to tell me what that's about?"

He stutters and looks around. Apparently, I've struck a nerve. I lock my eyes on him and stand stiffer.

"Okay, okay. I don't want to go to jail again."

I round the pile of sawdust so I'm standing within a few inches of Homer. Then I toy with the handcuffs on my belt. He flinches.

"Look, if you cooperate with me and tell me what's going on with Samuel, we can work together and keep you out of jail."

He nods rapidly.

"All right, then. Get in my car, and let's talk."

Homer and I walk side by side to the cop car. Before I say anything, he gets in the back. That's all I need to know he's guilty of something and willing to help.

I'm barely in my seat when he spills his story.

"It's not pills or nothing, but I've been making moonshine for years. Really good moonshine. I get special requests for everything from strawberry to jalapeño flavored."

"That's weird."

"Nah, it's awesome. You should try—"

He shuts his mouth when I raise an eyebrow.

"Careful. Remember who you're talking to."

Homer rubs his unshaven face and sighs. "All right, so Samuel knows I want to own a liquor store, but can't 'cause of the dry county and all."

"And because selling moonshine is illegal."

"It is?" His jaw drops.

I nod. "In the state of Alabama, yes."

"Shoooot. You don't say." He scratches his chin, as if rethinking his whole business.

"So back to you telling me what Samuel has to do with this so I don't arrest you."

He snaps back into focus. "Samuel knew I was wanting to open a liquor store. He told me Vernon was more likely open to making the county wet than you. If I get people to vote for Vernon, then he'd return the favor by sending me moonshine customers."

"He told you that just now?"

"The moonshine part, he did. He'd already told me the wet-county part." Homer jerks his head, then continues. "I can be kinda loud, so he wanted to meet privately where nobody would hear." He chuckles. "That's before we knew you was squatting in my favorite spitting spot."

I frown, and his chuckle ends. "Sorry about that, Sheriff."

"Apology accepted." I keep my face stern.

"But that's pretty much it. Samuel didn't drink any 'shine or nothing like that."

For the first time in my life, I'm disappointed someone isn't guilty of something. Namely, Samuel. I'm not sure what that says about me.

"I appreciate you telling me this, Homer. I'd like to think you'll come to me with any further information on this while I'm sheriff."

A lump forms in my throat when "while" seeps out. Like it or not, I have to get used to the fact that I might not be soon.

"Does this mean I can still sell it?"

"No! It means you tell me if someone comes to you from Samuel wanting to buy it."

He huffs. "Man! What am I supposed to do with all that I made up already—most custom orders?"

"I shouldn't say this, but there are several local fairs that judge moonshine. While it's illegal to sell the stuff, it's not illegal to enter it into a fair for judging. You can transport it to competitions and hopefully win some prize money."

"That's it?"

I shrug. "Or go to jail for peddling an illegal substance and spitting Skoal on my shoulder."

"I like your idea."

"As you should, big dog."

Ashley

Not to be dramatic, but this weekend about did me in.

Saturday was wild at the bank with everyone coming in last minute to cash checks for the weekend. That came on the heels of Homer's epic entrance and my email.

Oh, the email. I spent the rest of the day crafting the perfect response in my head. Then I stewed over whether to send it on Saturday or wait until today. Sending Saturday would let them know I'm prompt. But would it be too prompt since they sent it on Friday evening? I didn't want to send it on Sunday, since the older generation deems that disrespectful.

If they don't want us cutting grass on Sundays, why would sending a work-related email be any different?

I spent all Saturday stressing over the email, all Sunday after church crafting it, then finally hit Send this morning.

And all day, I've waited for a response.

Now I'm in the signal pit at Daisy's house, where there isn't enough cell service to tempt me to check my email. Maybe that's part of what makes goat yoga so relaxing?

I'm reaching for a mat when someone touches my hand. My eyes trail a tight T-shirt to the jawline I've become so fond of lately. Bradley.

"Hello, there." He grins. "Allow me." He pulls the mat I'm holding and another one from the bin.

I follow him to the back of the room like I'm in a trance. He is one more iron in the fire of my complicated mind. Every time I'd draft a new email, I'd think of Bradley and how I'd miss him if I move.

But my parents raised me to believe if something is meant to be, it will happen. I shouldn't hold myself back from anything to follow a guy. The beauty of moving away is that I'd start fresh.

"There you go." Bradley pats my mat and rolls his out beside it.

"Thanks." I smile and remind myself to relax. "Did you have a good weekend?"

"Yeah." He huffs tiredly. "I worked most of it, but it was good. How about you?"

"Yes." Not a total lie. It wasn't bad, just confusing.

"Okay, everyone." Daisy rubs the back of her goat's ears. "Let's get started."

The goat slides out from under her hand as if right on cue. A strand of hair mohawks on his head, helping him live up to the name Mullet. Most of the goats wander among us students, but he stays with Daisy throughout the workout. She treats him more like a dog, and he behaves as a loyal pet.

I lengthen my legs in front of me and reach for my toes. Bradley does the same, and I watch him from the corner of my eye. His biceps twist when he strains to try and reach his toes. I try not to think of him too fondly, or it will make the possibility of Birmingham that much harder.

Watching Bradley beside me with his flexing muscles and flirty smirks does nothing to keep him off my mind. But it does help me relax. I follow the motions Daisy leads us through, sharing glances with him when I bend his way. It's the most fun I've had since opening that email, and I'm sad when the class ends.

People make small talk as we clean our mats, and a few

mention the election. Nothing controversial—thank God!—, but to comment on how cute Trixie was at the debate or to wish Bradley luck.

He takes his time cleaning his mat, and I sense that he's hanging around to talk to me. Carolina is the last to leave after chatting about a potential party after the election.

I thank Daisy for the class and linger by the door. My theory is proven correct when Bradley grabs the handle and opens it for me. He walks me to my car and smiles at the otherwise empty parking area. Unless you count Daisy's car and her many farm animals milling around.

"Ashley, I've got to tell you something."

I blink up at him, suddenly nervous.

"I can't share details, but Samuel is involved in more sneakiness than I thought. I want you to be careful if you have to be alone with him."

I nod. Despite Samuel's arrogant control tendencies, I can't imagine him hurting me. Still, the very idea of him being dangerous makes a change of scenery all the more important.

"Bradley, I need to tell you something too." I stare at my feet and swallow. Although I don't owe him an explanation, I don't want to blindside him if I move.

"What? You can tell me anything."

His encouraging tone gives me courage to continue. I look him in the eye and get it over with. "I may be interviewing for a job in Birmingham."

"Birmingham, Alabama?"

I laugh. "Well, it's not Birmingham, England."

He sighs. "I guess that would be worse."

"This is something that was in the works before I got to know you better. A big bank I have connections with."

I search for more words, but he pulls me in for a hug. His arms wrap around my shoulders, and I rest my head against his chest. He smells like sweat and goat hair, but I don't mind. I wrap my arms around his waist, not wanting to leave.

"You don't owe me anything," he whispers. "Always do what's best for you and never regret it."

I nod slowly against his chest and mumble a thank you.

After a few more seconds in his warm embrace, I pull back and kiss him on the cheek. His lips curve sadly, and he opens my door. I climb in the car, and he hovers over it, smiling. "Remember, if you ever need me, I'm just a cowboy emoji away."

A sad, strained laugh comes out of me as he backs away and blows me a kiss. I drive down Daisy's road, blinking back a few stray tears. For all Birmingham has to offer, I don't think I'll find another Bradley.

CHAPTER NINETEEN

Bradley

Every year, the local elementary schools have a week to focus on D.A.R.E.—Drug Abuse Resistance Education. They have different dress-up days and do other things, and end with a speech from yours truly.

I normally take a PowerPoint and talk about how we identify drugs and bust manufacturers. Normal stuff to try and scare them straight before they go crooked. Today, however, I have something even better to grab their attention.

"Trixie." I purse my lips and make a kissing sound. She comes running and hops in the passenger seat. The kids are going to love her.

She must sense this isn't an average ride along, because she mounts her front paws on the dash and stares through the windshield with anticipation. I laugh, wishing I were that excited to go talk to eight-year-olds about the dangers of marijuana and meth.

Not much has excited me since Ashley said she might be moving.

I would love for her to stay, but I can't sound too clingy. She owes me nothing, and I'm nothing to her. If we had more time together, I'd hope I could remedy that. Which brings me back to her needing to decide without my meddling.

Trixie wags her tail when we pull in front of Apple Cart Elementary School. At least one girl in my life is happy.

"Hold on, girl." I warn Trixie to not be too friendly when I let her out of the car.

Principal Dingle greets us at the door with a goofy grin. "Good morning, sheriff."

"Morning." I nod toward the dog. "This is Miss Trixie."

"Yes, I saw her at the debate." He adjusts his glasses and bends to pet her.

I wait awkwardly with my supplies in one hand and a leash in the other while he talks to Trixie like old ladies talk to babies. He makes over her for several minutes before standing. Then he transitions to professional mode in less than a second. It's a little intimidating—even for me.

"The kids will be in the gym. If you want to go ahead and set up, it's open."

I squint my eyes. All the doors are supposed to be locked at all times.

"Mark is already in there."

I nod. The school resource officer is very green as a cop and an adult. I make a mental note to check up on him randomly.

"Thanks, Principal."

"Please, call me Dingle."

"I'd rather not."

He grins again. "You're too respectful. What we need in leadership. I like it."

He reaches out his lanky hand and pats me on the shoulder. Trixie shows her teeth, until I tug at her leash to let her know it's okay. I don't have the heart to tell him Dingle makes me think of berries.

Trixie sniffs all the way to the gym. She will make a fine drug dog one day.

I pet her head approvingly when we reach the gym door. I open it to Mark shooting a basketball. "Mark!"

He drops the ball mid-shot and stands at attention. I shake my head. "If you're gonna do something like this, lock the door first."

He nods. "Yes, sir, Sheriff." He retrieves the ball and puts it in a closet.

I set my box of fake drug samples to the side and look for a chair. Photos are great, but it helps if I can replicate something tangible and pass it around for the kids to see.

Mark gets us both a chair from the closet and finds a small mat for Trixie. I use this as a teachable moment and position Mark by the door.

I've barely sat down when the bell rings. A woman comes over the intercom immediately afterward, instructing all classes to make their way to the gym.

Within ten minutes, Dingle has brought me a lapel mic and the gym is packed with kids and teachers. I turn the mic on and try not to think about Ashley going undercover. I've put more stress on her than I should have, and I hope that isn't influencing her decision to move.

Trixie acts like the perfect pup she is, sniffing the sugar disguised as a drug when I ask her to. I explain how this is really sugar, but that some drugs would look like this packaging. One kid gets in trouble by a teacher for trying to sample it, and I'm reminded why I usually bring photos.

At the end of my presentation, I ask if anyone has questions. Several hands go up around the room. I skip past some of the most eager little kids. Intuition tells me they'd just ask to pet Trixie.

Not to profile, but I choose a quiet boy with his hand half-raised. He asks if the dog tasted the drugs to see if they were real or sugar. Fair enough question for an elementary kid, but still about Trixie. I explain a little about how a dog uses its nose more than other senses.

"Any more questions?"

Almost every hand raises. I exhale deeply. "Any more questions that aren't about dogs?"

Half the hands go down. I glance toward the oldest kids and point to a blonde girl with a bored-to-death look. No way she's going to ask about the dog.

And she doesn't.

"Are you married?"

I chuckle. "Aren't you a little young for me?"

"I wasn't asking for me. But aren't you a little old to spend so much time with a dog?"

What a little . . . I frown.

"I can spend all my time with a dog and still be married."

"Well, are you?"

I squirm in my chair and slide my hand away from Trixie's back. Several teachers stare at me to see how I'll respond. One middle-aged woman winks my way. Dingle starts to stand as if he's about to bring all back to order.

I stand before he does and decide to set the record straight. "I was on track to marry a girl, but I was immature and took her for granted. She married someone else." I put my hands on my hips, a little shocked at admitting all this in front of an elementary school.

"For a long time, I thought I'd never like another girl like that. Then I met someone." I sigh. "But I'm afraid I ruined that too."

"How?" the girl sitting beside the blonde one asks.

I drop my hands and plop back in the folding chair. Trixie senses my sadness and rests her head on my knee. "Sometimes I love too hard and push too much."

I look at Trixie and run my hand over her back. Then I stare back at the kids. "Moral of the story is nobody will love you more than a dog." I snap my fingers. "Oh, and don't do drugs."

Ashley

Three or more Smart Money Credit Unions could fit inside Bama State Bank. The first floor sent me to the third floor for my interview.

The last time I was in an elevator was with Bradley in the Baptist church.

This one is much newer, with mirrored walls. I adjust my skirt and try not to think about Bradley. Then my phone buzzes.

Good luck on your interview.

He follows that with a cowboy emoji. I have to hold back tears, even though it makes me laugh.

. . .

Thanks. Have a good weekend.

I sign my text with a heart emoji. It's safe to say I love Bradley at least on some level, but I don't dare say it. He can interpret the heart however he wants.

I silence my phone and shove it in my purse as the elevator dings. It opens across from a lobby with a desk out front. The third-floor lobby is minuscule compared to the rest of the building. The woman behind the desk looks up when I approach.

"Hi, I'm Ashley Armstrong. I have an interview at ten."

She smiles. "Yes, you will be meeting with Mrs. Jones and our branch president. I'll notify them you're here. Have a seat."

"Thanks."

I smile and sit in one of the four chairs surrounding a small coffee table decorated with finance magazines and a bowl of mints. I didn't notice downstairs, but I bet a place like this serves mints instead of suckers.

What would it be like to not have Paul come in and stash all the suckers?

No, I refuse to get sentimental over Paul and those blasted suckers. I choke back yet another tear.

This bank and this city could change my life—for the better. Even if I don't like Birmingham, they have several branches and even more contacts at other large banks. A clean start away from all things Samuel, including Apple Cart, might be the best thing for me.

"Miss Armstrong."

I stand and smile at the young woman now in the lobby.

"Hi. Mr. Osmore and Mrs. Jones are ready for you. Follow me."

She leads me past the elevator down a long hallway. At

the end is a glass door. We pass through it and another small lobby to another shorter hallway, ending at the last door.

I was wrong before. Five Smart Moneys could fit in this building, minimum.

"Carlos Osmore, Bank Branch President" stares at me from a gold plaque on the door. The girl opens it and waves me inside. I pass her and fix my eyes on the two well-dressed people sitting at the end of the room.

"Thank you, Liv," Mr. Osmore says. His voice booms though the large space. The door shuts behind me, making me flinch. Somehow, I will my legs to work and take me to the massive desk across the room.

The only sounds are my heels on the wood and my heart pounding. Hopefully they can't hear my heart. Mrs. Jones smiles at me, calming my nerves a bit. We emailed a few times this week, and she made me feel at ease the time we'd met in person.

"Good to see you again, Ashley."

"You too."

I smile at her bright gray hair grazing the shoulders of her red blazer. Her look and demeanor are goals. And her career.

"Ashley, you come highly recommended by Roberta."

"Thank you." I say it to Mr. Osmore, but glance at Mrs. Jones with gratitude.

He wastes no time going over my resume and all the responsibilities of the lead loan officer position. I love that he gets straight to the point and is all business. He then gives me time to ask questions. However, what he says next impresses me most.

"You remind me of my granddaughter. She's a very deep thinker and asks good questions. That seems lost in your generation."

"Thank you."

How great would it be to have a boss who actually wants

to mentor me instead of hit on me? Samuel would never call me a deep thinker! As far as he's concerned, my head exists to hold my hair and eyelashes.

After I've asked everything I can imagine about the job, I thank them both for the interview.

"We appreciate you coming in. I'll let Roberta show you around her department before you leave." Mr. Osmore stands after I do and shakes my hand.

Mrs. Jones leads me to the hall and stops a few doors down. "This is my office."

She opens a door to a cozy, upscale room with a nice view of downtown. Cliché as it sounds, I now get the appeal of a corner office.

"Next door is an office housing our loan-processing team. Liv interns for me and will be available a few more months for whomever takes my place."

I nod, and Mrs. Jones smiles. "I can't read his mind, but I can see Carlos likes you. The granddaughter comment is a great compliment."

"I thought so." I relax some.

"I'll let you meet my team before you go."

We walk next door, and I glance back at her office. It's hard to imagine myself in a big city after growing up and working in a rural area all my life. But as a little girl, I was fascinated with living somewhere I could shop to my heart's content.

Mrs. Jones introduces me to three people, not counting Liv, who all report directly to her. They all supervise other people as well. At our bank, I work alongside the head teller to help anyone who needs it, and we all report to Samuel.

Here I would be over more people, but also have the bank president and VP and HR over me. Samuel being nowhere in that equation is the most refreshing of all.

After a few minutes and more questions, we head to the elevator.

"I'll walk you out." Mrs. Jones smiles and hits the elevator button.

I stare at the door as it opens and follow her inside. Another man joins us on the second floor, so we ride in silence. Not until we're in the main floor lobby does she speak freely.

"Ashley, I think you'd be perfect for this job. To be totally transparent, we have more interviews, and there are a lot of people up for it. I'll put in a good word for you with Carlos."

"You don't know how much I appreciate that." I look into her kind eyes and wish there were a way I could repay her.

"I hope to see you back here soon." She touches my arm and smiles, then heads toward the elevator.

I glance around the massive space one more time before walking to the parking lot. On a positive note, I could totally picture myself here. On the negative, I can't picture anyone from Apple Cart County here with me. In particular, Bradley.

Would I be okay with that?

CHAPTER TWENTY

Bradley

I've been a lot of weird places around this county, but Homer Giles's place has to be in the top three. Paul's store always holds steady in the top spot, and the motel/liquor store/restaurant on the county line is always second.

"Congratulations, Homer. You beat Waffle House."

"Huh?" Homer gives me a dumbfounded look, and I realize I said that out loud.

"Never mind. What is Samuel planning now?"

"Have a seat." He pulls two five-gallon buckets closer to us and flips them upside down.

I sit on one and take in the surroundings. My first thought is *what a huge rabbit*, so I stand for a closer look. "Is that a kangaroo in that pen?"

"Yeah, I have five of them right now."

"Do you breed them or something?"

He shakes his head. "They fight." He smiles. "I make lots of money on folks coming out to watch them box, and—"

I cross my arms and shake my head. He stops talking when he sees my reaction. "Is that illegal?"

I nod my head.

"Oh." He rubs his chin and shrugs.

I sit back on my bucket and make a mental note to shut down any future kangaroo fights before I leave.

"Samuel is coming out here to check out my setup. He keeps talking about all this stuff we can do when Vernon gets in, but Vernon doesn't have any idea."

"What do you mean?"

He shrugs again. "Samuel was really interested in my 'shine, and also my kangaroos. I'm not sure why."

"He's an odd dude. You know he owns a rabbit."

"A fighting rabbit?"

"Hardly." I chuckle, then get back to business. "What's Vernon's deal in this?"

"I don't know."

"Tell you what, if you can get Samuel to talk when he's here, I won't press charges for any past kangaroo fights." I lift a finger. "But you have to get a vet out here to check them out and never fight them again."

"What about the event I have on Facebook already?"

"A fight?"

"Yeah, it's tomorrow night."

"Cancel it." I stand and put my hands on my hips. "You're on thin ice, Homer. Play straight and get Samuel to talk for me, or you're the one who will be fighting in jail soon."

He salutes me.

I shake my head. "Give me some notice before your next meeting with Samuel so I can prepare."

"Yes, sir."

I climb in my car and pick up my phone once I'm down his dirt road. "Hey, Natalie? This is Bradley Manning."

"Oh hey, is everything good with Trixie?"

"Wonderful. We'll be at scheduled training this week like always."

"Great. She's doing so well."

"Yeah." I sigh. "So how do you feel about kangaroos?"

"Did you say kangaroos?"

"Yeah. Keep an open mind, I'll explain more in person when we're there."

I don't expect her to train kangaroos, but I believe she would be a good option to house them until we find a zoo or something more permanent than Homer's yard.

"Okay." She laughs.

"See you at training."

"Okay, Bradley."

"Bye." I hang up and find Vernon's contact. First thing I did when he announced his candidacy was find everything I could on him. That, of course, included his phone number.

"Hello?"

"Hey. Bradley Manning."

A long breath comes across the line.

"Look, I'm not trying to start anything. I just wanted to say best of luck to you and see how things are going."

"Fine, I guess. I haven't been campaigning, really."

"If you win, I'd hope we can still work together to keep everything running smoothly around here."

Another long breath. I wait for him to speak.

"Bradley, I've always looked up to you."

"I'm honored, really." I can hear the sincerity in his voice.

"I'm running because someone convinced me it would be a good move for my career and help my family."

"I see." He doesn't say who, but I suspect that someone is Samuel. "Well, may the best man win."

"I agree. Good luck to you."

I hear a baby in the background. It would be like Samuel to manipulate a young guy trying to provide for his family. I best end this call before I say something I shouldn't. "To you too, big dog."

Now that I know Vernon has nothing against me, I can assume it's all Samuel. This makes me want to catch him that much more.

If I can get to Samuel through Homer, and possibly Vernon, I no longer need Ashley's help. At least concerning the case. On a personal level, I've been experiencing Ashley withdrawals.

Ashley

Samuel didn't ask for details when I put in to take off Friday and Saturday. I assumed he was caught up in himself too much to care. That is until this morning. He's acting way too kind and accommodating.

He has to know I'm considering another job.

Speaking of Samuel, he smiles at me when I look up from my desk. If he thinks playing sweet will be the deciding factor in my staying at his bank, he's clueless. I've known Samuel long enough to experience all his moods.

My smile widens when the door swings open and a tan cowboy hat dips inside. Like a cheesy romance-movie hero, Bradley raises his head and slowly removes his sunglasses. Our eyes meet, and I catch myself sighing.

Nerves swirl in my stomach like tennis shoes in a dryer as

he approaches my desk.

"Good morning, ma'am." He tips his hat, causing me to blush.

If anything could convince me to stay, it would be that.

I clear my throat. We haven't spoken in person since before my interview. "Good morning. Can I help you with anything?"

"Maybe." He takes a seat in front of me. "Have you heard anything yet?"

I cut my eyes toward Glenda, who is nearby sorting papers. "Let's go out here."

I circle my desk and head for the door with Bradley behind me. Once we're outside, I speak freely. "I haven't heard anything." I stare at the ground, my stomach now fully knotted from tossing an extra pair of shoes—or concern—on top of the previous dilemma.

"I'm sure they loved you." He grins.

The tennis shoes hit my heart and tumble back down my gut. I bite my bottom lip. "They had a lot of people apply and are interviewing several."

"So? She reached out to you personally. That's got to be good, right?"

I shrug. "I'm confused."

"Did you not like it there?"

"I did. It's just . . ." I want to say *you're not there*, but instead, I go with, ". . . different."

"Most everywhere is different from Apple Cart County."

"True."

We share a laugh, and my tension eases a bit. "It pays a good bit more than my job here."

"So does the mines."

I roll my eyes. "Could you really picture me wearing a helmet, swinging a pickax?"

His grin turns mischievous.

"Never mind, don't answer that," I say.

"You have to factor in the cost of living in Birmingham."

"Yeah, I thought of that."

In fact, I've thought of everything. Sad to say, the one determining factor might be to escape Samuel.

"I really want to get away from working under Samuel."

"I understand." He frowns. "Is that the only reason you want to move?"

"I'm getting a little old to live with my parents."

"You can rent a house around here like I do."

I waver my head. "That might be an option, but it's mainly Samuel."

Bradley exhales. "With any luck, none of us will have to put up with him much longer."

My eyes widen.

He puts a hand on my shoulder, and the tennis shoes inside me instantly stop tumbling. "Do you need me to help with anything?" I ask.

He shakes his head and lets his hand slide from my shoulder. "I've used you enough. I don't want to put you in any more harm's way. I should be able to get what I need on my own."

I tell myself to focus on the fact that he wants to protect me, but all my mind wants to dwell on are the words "used you." Is that all he was doing?

I want to ask for clarification, but my mouth won't let me. And Samuel sticks his head out the door. "Ashley, what are you doing? I need you to work."

Bradley nods to him, then smiles at me as I pull the door wider and rush past Samuel to my desk.

In a split second, I've realized two things. One, Samuel is a total turd who I can't keep working for. And two, I don't have enough clarity or history with Bradley to allow him to affect my job decision either way.

CHAPTER TWENTY-ONE

Bradley

Roughly twenty young women in shiny dresses parade in front of me.

No, this isn't the most interesting police lineup ever. And I'm not at Sparrow's Booby Trap drowning my sorrows. I'm judging the Miss Applesauce Pageant that happens every fall in our county.

Ashley signed me up to judge because she said it would connect me with the community in a new way. How ironic that the only woman I care to look at would volunteer me to look at a whole group of pretty girls younger than herself. I blame Becki for planting the idea in her head since the newspaper sponsors this pageant.

I do my best to focus on the pageant instead of wishing I were watching Ashley strut across the stage. It's actually a tractor trailer decorated with ferns and white Christmas lights, but it serves the purpose of giving them a tall platform.

I'm in a folding chair beside the mayor and two women from out of town I met a few minutes earlier. The girls exit down steps placed at the end of the trailer. Becki calls out the first contestant, and she goes back up the steps.

For the next half hour, we watch as every girl walks in front of us. I score them one to ten on smile, dress, and walk. I'm probably not judging the dress part right. I imagine every dress on Ashley and rate it how I think she would make it look. Every dress gets a high score, except for one covered in feathers.

The only place I can imagine her wearing that is a charity ball for Top Chick Foods.

They come out one more time in a group. Mrs. Genene, better known as one of the county's busybodies, comes to the stage with a bowl in one hand and a mic in the other.

"We have a list of random questions submitted from the community. Each contestant will answer one," Becki explains.

This should be good. I lean back and fold my arms. We have a place on the scoresheet to rate their answers. That doesn't really seem fair if they get different questions, but the last time I judged anything remotely close to this was a wet T-shirt contest at a frat house.

"Contestant number one, please select a question from the bowl and hand it to Mrs. Genene."

Genene smiles and waves with the hand holding the mic, causing it to squeak. She winces and lowers it.

A brunette in a red dress steps forward and fumbles around in the fishbowl. She hands a slip of paper to Genene.

"Okay." She unfolds the paper and holds it out to read. "How do you like your steak?"

"Medium rare, because it's very flavorful, but with a little grit around the edges." The brunette smiles widely.

I can get behind that answer. I give her a nine.

Genene says, "Good answer," before Becki calls the next contestant, and she continues to do so each time. I pinch the bridge of my nose and sigh. It's like watching an episode of *Family Feud* with better-looking contestants.

What we should really rate are the questions. It's like going to a town debate, but weirder, as there is an anonymous factor behind it.

Some of my favorite questions are:

How many Dollar Generals do you think our county needs?

If you could create a candle, what scent would you make it? (That had to come from Daisy.)

What will you do with the prize money if you win?

Do you have a boyfriend?

I sincerely hope the boyfriend question came from a fellow high schooler. Having gone through a recent debate, I sympathize with these girls answering the whole town's random thoughts. And they're doing it in uncomfortable shoes, without a loyal dog by their side.

We turn our papers over to Genene, who takes them to a local accountant set up with a laptop.

"While the question scores are being tallied, let's meet our judges," Becki says.

The women both have pageant things in their bios, making them a hundred times more qualified to judge this thing than the mayor and me. Becki talks about Mayor Lewis long enough to calculate every score on every question ever asked. He stands proudly, waving to the crowd while she turns pages through his resume.

She saved me for last. I turn around and wave to the crowd, giving her a nod of approval when she mentions my run for reelection.

Genene returns a piece of paper to Becki. Then she hurries to a table of trophies on the back of the trailer. A girl in a shorter dress and crown comes out and walks the walk the contestants did. Becki introduces her as last year's winner.

When she stops in the back by Genene, Becki starts to announce the results. I'm rooting for the blonde that reminds me the most of Ashley.

She gets a trophy, but not the crown. The brunette in the red dress wins Applesauce Queen. Must be the steak question. I can't argue with that.

The other girl sticks a crown on her head, and Genene hands her flowers. She walks and waves as the crowd behind me claps. I remember the year my high school girlfriend won this. The trailer was much older, and she almost tripped on a loose board doing her victory walk.

Becki thanks everyone for coming and directs the girls off the so-called stage for photos by an antique tractor display. Jillian lifts her camera and positions the winners with different poses in front of a John Deere.

People start gathering their lawn chairs and scattering around the fairgrounds. The women judges are long gone, and the mayor is mingling with everyone. Kyle pulls beside our table in a side-by-side. He climbs out and begins folding chairs. I stare at the stage decorations in a slight daze.

"You gonna get up today?" he asks.

I jerk my head to him staring at me with his hand on the back of my chair. "My bad."

I stand and let him take it. Then I break down the table to help him out. We work in silence a few minutes, taking down the table on the stage. Genene comes by and gives orders for what we can and can't touch of the decorations.

"Kyle?"

"Yeah?" He tosses some white net stuff off the trailer and faces me.

"I'm worried."

"About what?"

"Ashley." I sigh. "She interviewed for a job in Birmingham."

"Oh, the Bama State Bank job."

"How did you know?"

He stares at the sky and exhales. "Daisy heard it from Adrianne, who heard it from Carolina, and I forget the rest." He looks at me.

"What if she takes it?"

He shrugs.

I cross my arms and focus on the balloons by my feet. "I let one woman move away. I don't want to let another."

Kyle frowns. "Want my opinion?"

"Well, yeah, big dog, that's why I asked."

"You can't expect her to stay for you when you're not her boyfriend, and it's selfish if you ask her to."

"I know."

"Good."

"Then where does that leave me?"

"Here, in Apple Cart." He fans his hand to the side. "If it's meant to be, she'll stay or come back, or you'll move. Go on with your life, and if it's supposed to happen, it will."

I nod, then chuckle.

"What?" Kyle asks.

"When did you get so smart?"

He tosses a wad of lights my way. I cover my head and let them hit the trailer. Genene hears them land and turns to me tossing wads of cotton at Kyle.

"Gentlemen?" She arches a brow.

We both mumble a "sorry." Then we get back to work.

I hope Ashley ends up staying, because I couldn't imagine myself living somewhere that doesn't parade queens around on tractor trailers.

Ashley

On my way back from lunch, my phone rings. It's an unknown number so I let it go to voicemail.

I continue driving, letting it ring. My car speaker is set to play any voicemails as they come in, and I fully expect to hear a telemarketer. I almost run off the road when the HR woman from Bama State Bank comes over the phone.

This is the call I've waited on for three days, or five if you count the weekend. I pull onto the nearest side road and listen again.

It's lunchtime, but maybe she will get my call. My finger shakes as I hit Redial. She answers, and I hold my stomach. I didn't realize this would be so nerve-racking.

"This is Ashley Armstrong," I manage to say.

"Yes, Miss Armstrong. Did you get my voicemail?"

"I did. I was driving."

"I can go over more specific details of the package, but we'd like to offer you the lead loan officer position."

"Could you give me more details?"

I shock myself with this response. I wanted to say yes right away, but I need a few seconds to think.

My heart races. Bradley's face flashes in my mind.

No. I can't base my decision on a guy I've kissed a few times and helped with what may or may not be a criminal case. I can date him long-distance if we want. Besides, my family will still want me to visit often.

I half listen to the salary I was already quoted, followed by 401K and health insurance explanations. By the time she stops speaking, I'm confident I can accept. Not because of the benefits package, but because I know I need to base my future on something besides a chance with Bradley.

"That sounds great."

"Awesome. We can connect over email about a time to come in and fill out all the paperwork."

"Thank you." I relax my shoulders.

I did it. I found a good job in a big city, and I'll have enough money to move out. I'm officially an adult.

We end the call, and I take a minute to let it all soak in.

The drive back to the bank excites me more than a drive to the beach. I practically float through the front door and don't stop until I'm in front of Samuel's office. I knock on his closed door, and wait for him to say, "Come in."

With the confidence of a lottery winner, I march into his office. Not so much because of the salary increase, but more because of the power over my future. One that will not involve Samuel in any way.

"I'm leaving." I force myself to keep a straight face for the sake of staying professional.

"Where are you going?" He stares at my purse still on my shoulder.

"Birmingham."

"You need to put in a request to be gone that long."

"Yeah, about that." My face twitches as I fight smiling. "I'm not going today. I'm going for good."

He lifts his eyes from his computer screen and studies my face. He's confused, and I love it. But there's no use dragging this out.

"I'm moving."

His eyebrows shoot up.

"Consider this my two weeks' notice."

He coughs and half chokes, then composes himself

enough to speak. "You need to draft a formal resignation letter for this to be valid."

"Absolutely." I turn on my heel and walk out, not bothering to close his door.

I've had a letter drafted in a folder on my desktop for more than a year. All that's missing is the date. If that's not enough evidence I need to take this job, I don't know what is.

Typing in today's date at the top seems surreal. I print two copies in case Samuel rips it up. Then I email it to him for good measure.

I'm shocked to see he hasn't shut his door. In fact, I don't think he's moved at all. He sits at his desk, staring ahead like he's frozen.

"Samuel, I have my resignation letter." I walk to his desk. "I also emailed it to you."

He doesn't move. I slide it on his desk and take a step back.

"Get out." His voice is clipped and low.

"Pardon me?"

"Get out," he says louder.

I back toward the door, a little scared to turn my back to him. Between his dazed expression and stern tone, I don't know what he'll do.

My body tenses when I sit at my desk. I've barely rebooted my computer and opened the loan programs when Samuel's voice booms beside me. "Get out!"

Everyone in the bank goes silent. Glenda stops beside me and drops an armful of folders. I flinch when they hit the ground.

"Let me finish this loan I started before lunch."

"No, get out now."

I stand, challenging him. "I put in an official notice. I need to finish the things I've started for my clients."

"You'll get paid for the two weeks, but I can't see you here anymore."

"What about our customers?"

He scoffs. "You think I can't take care of it?"

There's no good way I could answer that. I glance around at the tellers, Glenda, and the customers. All eyes are on my exchange with Samuel, and I can't blame them. There's only one response that won't start World War III.

"I'll clean out my desk."

A hand goes on my shoulder, offering comfort. I turn to Glenda tearing up. I offer her a sympathetic face, then squeeze her hand. Samuel stands a few feet away, arms crossed, proving he isn't moving until I'm gone.

I sigh and open a desk drawer. There isn't much here I own. A few personal items in a drawer and some photos and desk decor. It takes me all of five minutes to gather everything.

The tellers give me sad eyes, as does Ms. Ethel, who stands at the first station. She gives Samuel another look that doesn't bless his heart. I want to high-five her, but restrain.

"I'll see you all around. I've enjoyed getting to know every one of you."

Glenda wraps her arms around my neck, squishing my desk plant against my blouse. I don't care what it does to my clothes. If my arms weren't full, I'd hug her back.

I choke back a tear and head for the door with Samuel close behind. Shockingly, he has the decency to open it for me. I slide out sideways, my belongings in tow. The bank door closes behind me, shutting a chapter on my life.

An invigorating force rises inside me with the realization that I no longer have to answer to Samuel. Hopefully it will help me unlock and open my car door with an armful of junk.

CHAPTER TWENTY-TWO

Bradley

"I'm nervous." Homer spits to the side, thankfully missing me this time.

"You have nothing to worry about, big dog. I'll be hidden even better than before. That's why we're doing this."

I hold up the mic and clip it to his collar. Totally different effect than when I clipped it on Ashley. Does he even have a collarbone? It's hard to tell under the neck and chest hair meeting.

"It's on, so you don't have to worry about anything. Act natural and talk like always."

He swipes at his hair as if the mic includes a camera. But we do have a game cam hidden nearby to get any footage I might need.

"I'll be over here, hidden."

I find a spot several yards back behind some blocks of hay. Far enough where none of the animals can spot me.

Then I pull down the mask to my ghillie suit and sit on the ground. Homer's yard offers plenty of places to spy. It would be a great place for a game of hide-and-seek, though I'd recommend getting a tetanus shot first.

He stares at the pile of hay, so I talk in his ear. "Don't look for me. Act like I'm not here."

He jumps at first, then gives me a thumbs-up.

"Remember, you can be pardoned if you do what I said."

He salutes me, and I shake my head. This might've been a bad idea.

I settle farther behind the hay and make myself comfortable. Samuel's car creeps down the dirt road and parks in front of Homer's house. He climbs out and twists his wrist, causing his watch to catch the setting sun.

"Homer, how are you?" He shakes Homer's hand.

"Good." Homer's eyes cut toward the hay.

"Stop looking for me," I whisper-yell.

He darts his gaze to the trees behind Samuel.

"I've got you more work."

"You do?" Homer beams.

I hope he realizes being an informant doesn't include going through with illegal business.

Samuel nods. "There's a group out of Mississippi wanting to buy your moonshine in bulk. I can run some recipes and business transactions through the bank to have a paper trail. That way you can sell to your heart's content."

"What's in it for you?"

"What do you mean by that?" Samuel chuckles.

"You always give me a condition like getting Vernon elected or sharing profits with you."

"Nothing. This is from one businessman to another."

Homer glances my way. I make a buzzing sound in his ear. He slaps the side of his head and curses.

"What's wrong?" Samuel scrunches his forehead.

"Blasted bee I need to kill." He glares at the hay, and I give up. I only need Samuel to confess a few more things, then it won't matter what Homer does or says.

"So you don't want votes or profits or nothing?"

Samuel shakes his head. "All I want is your business."

"My business. Like personalized 'shine?"

"No." Samuel laughs. "I only drink the finest wines and champagnes," he boasts. "I want to use your business to help the bank."

"What do you mean my business? I haven't started anything official."

"Exactly, and with my help, you won't need to." He snakes an arm around Homer's shoulder like they're best buds. "I'll even pay you to let me do your paperwork."

Homer removes his arm. This is getting so good. I inch closer like my favorite movie is playing, and Hangman comes out of nowhere to save the day.

"This ain't adding up," Homer says.

Samuel twists his watch and smirks. "It's simple, my friend. I take care of the paperwork, and you go about your business any way you want. I do it all the time with my side hustles."

"Side hustles?"

"A little sports betting." Samuel smirks proudly.

"I still don't get it."

Homer is asking all the right questions. Why didn't I think of recruiting him sooner? Probably because a logging hand with a part-time booze business didn't seem like the top recruit to help nail a dirty banker.

"Homer." Samuel pats his shoulder in a condescending way. "You don't have to understand. All you need to know is when I make money doing your paperwork, you get some money for free. You can put that back into your business or spend it as you wish. Then you won't need to worry about getting a loan. You can do whatever you want and have plenty of money to work with."

"So I get to have a 'shine business here in Apple Cart County?"

"Yes, but not officially."

"Then what?" Homer scratches his head.

I come off my knees to near standing. This is it.

"We name it something different, nothing to do with moonshine or anything against the law. An honorable business." His cheeks raise into a smile that would make a used car salesman envious. "I use business names all the time to fund my betting."

"Are you sure that's legal?"

"As long as we put the money back in the bank and then some, why wouldn't it be?"

It's my time to shine. I jump in front of the hay and jerk off my mask. Before Samuel knows what's coming, I'm whipping out handcuffs.

"You are under arrest. You have the right to remain silent. Anything you say can and will be used against you in a court of law. You have a right to an attorney. If you cannot afford an attorney, one will be appointed for you."

I lock the cuffs and pull him toward me.

"You set me up!" he yells in my face.

"And how many people have you set up?"

"This is the first person I've told about it."

I laugh. All the better. Those papers and records will prove he's done much more without anyone's consent.

Homer wipes sweat from his brow as I lead Samuel toward the hidden police car.

"It should be illegal how you hid out here like this."

"That's part of my job." I open the door and push him inside. "You're the one doing everything illegal."

I shut the door, then look back and salute Homer. He

holds up the mic and gives me a thumbs-up. I'll be back for that and the game cam later.

Samuel and I ride off into the sunset for his long-awaited date with a jail cell.

Ashley

"This unit has a gas stove, so you will need both gas and electric." Debra, the apartment manager, runs her hand across the countertop.

I glance around the kitchen until Carolina calls my attention to the living room. "Hey, there's a gas fireplace too. That would be nice."

"Is gas expensive?" I ask Debra.

"Not for something this size."

I'm checking out one-bedroom apartments close to the bank. Since I've never paid rent or utilities, I don't know what to expect. That's why I brought Carolina along. Well, that plus her decorative eye. She has a way of envisioning what a place will look like with my belongings.

"Can I look at the bedroom once more?"

"Of course." Debra smiles, and hangs back in the kitchen area.

Carolina follows me into the tiny bedroom. "The closet is a decent size for this room."

"I thought so too," I agree. "But there's no way all my bedroom furniture will fit in here."

"We can go thrifting for stuff and refinish it." Carolina's face lights up at the idea of a furniture project.

"It will have to be thrift store." I sigh. "It's hard to believe how much more I could afford in Apple Cart or Sparrow."

I'd looked into renting before. The upside was it costs much less than this. The downside was I had a much smaller paycheck than I will make in Birmingham.

Debra greets us when we reenter the main area. "Any more questions?"

"When do I need to let you know something?"

"The sooner, the better if you want one of the units with a fireplace. Due to regulations, only a few have that feature since they need to be ventless and up to code."

I nod. That is a nice feature. I imagine decorating the mantel for Christmas. "Thank you for showing us around today."

"You bet." She pulls a business card from her pocket. "This is my direct line and email. Call or send a message when you make a decision."

"Thank you." I take the card.

"Thanks," Carolina adds as we leave the unit.

She starts chattering about the structural difference in the three units we viewed. To me, the only difference was which side the bedroom was on and if it had a fake fireplace or extra window at the end of the living room.

My phone rings and I stare at Bradley's name. The last time we talked was when I stopped by to take a photo of him with Trixie for the campaign page I made on social media. I told him about taking the job, and he said he was happy for me. We hugged and promised to never lose touch.

That stung a little.

"Keep in touch" is more appropriate for distant relatives and old classmates. I don't want to just keep in touch with Bradley. But I knew this would likely be the outcome if I moved to Birmingham.

"Are you going to answer that?"

"Huh?" I stare at Carolina, then click my phone. "Hello?"

"Hey. I was preparing to leave a voicemail. Are you busy?"

"Not at the moment."

"I know I said I didn't need you anymore on the case, but we've had a big breakthrough."

"Really?"

Carolina hits the elevator button in front of us, and I lean against the wall. She gives me a nosy glance, but I ignore her. The elevator dings and I follow her inside.

"Samuel is currently in a holding cell awaiting a trial," Bradley says.

"Really?"

Carolina elbows me and mouths "what," but I brush her off.

"I wired Homer and used a camera to capture Samuel describing how he's been using those false documents to launder money for illegal sports betting."

"Wow."

The elevator door opens to a group of people. This cools Carolina for a bit. I slide to the corner, away from her.

"Yeah. I wanted to see if you'd maybe be available next Thursday."

"Thursday? Yeah, what time?"

"The trial starts at nine. I hope we don't need you as a witness, but just in case."

"Oh." My heart deflates.

As much as I want to help put Samuel away, I stupidly thought he was asking me out. Thursday isn't a traditional date night, but with Bradley's hours, it made sense.

"Sure. I'll be happy to help with whatever I can."

I genuinely mean that.

The elevator opens to the main floor. Carolina and I

allow the group to file off, then follow. She goes back to staring at me like she might pop if she doesn't get some answers. I hold up a finger to make her wait a little longer.

"Great. I'll be in touch about the details," Bradley answers.

In touch. I try not to take that phrase to heart. "Of course."

"Thanks, Ashley. And I really am happy for you with your new job. You're going to do great things."

"Thanks. Bye."

I hang up before he can say anything else suitable for a motivational poster you'd find in a middle-school counselor's office.

"What?" Carolina is literally jumping with anticipation.

"That was Bradley."

"I know. I saw your phone screen."

I sigh. "Samuel is in a holding cell."

"I know."

"What? How?"

She rolls her eyes. "You forget my brother is best friends with Jack, who's married to Bianca, who goes to the salon all the time."

"Okay?"

"News of this hit Adrianne's salon before I left my house to pick you up this morning."

"That's crazy."

"That's Apple Cart County."

I smile to myself, relieved that news can't possibly travel that quickly in a big city. At least not through the word-of-mouth method.

"The trial is next Thursday."

Carolina's eyes widen. "Could he, like, go to jail?"

I shrug. "I can't say he wouldn't deserve it."

Her eyes bug some more, and she twists a strand of her hair. "I can't believe we have a real crime in Apple Cart."

I laugh. "Carolina, Bradley busts up meth labs all the time."

"Yeah, but an actual smart crime." She jerks her head toward me, her jaw dropped. "What if we end up on *True Crime*?"

I shake my head and walk toward the apartment exit.

"What? Don't you think that would be something?" She chatters on excitedly. The crime aspect is the furthest thing from my mind.

I'm more concerned with what this will mean for all my friends at the credit union, for Bradley, and even Samuel. He is a horrible guy, but his poor family. Okay, so they are not technically poor. But I sympathize with anyone who has a family member going to jail.

I take a deep breath and follow Carolina to her car. She pauses talking and unlocks the doors.

"Man, it's a good thing you got out of the bank when you did," she says when we're inside.

"Yeah."

She shifts the conversation to lunch options. I comment here and there, although my appetite is gone. My mind is on my friends at the bank and all the people who come in each week.

Who knows what they will do to replace Samuel? His family does still own the branch.

CHAPTER TWENTY-THREE

Bradley

Apple Cart County folks come out in droves for three things: parades, Piggly Wiggly meat sales, and Samuel Covington's trial.

Everyone and their mother—literally—stares as I walk Samuel down the aisle of the courtroom toward the judge.

If the crowd isn't enough to intimidate Samuel, maybe Judge Wright will do it. He's old, big, and grumpy. The black robe hides his gut, giving him a tougher look. I doubt Samuel has seen him before since he doesn't go out in public.

Once I have Samuel seated by his lawyer, Judge Wright enters the room through his little door behind the stand. I make eye contact with the jury. Most of them are from Wisteria or don't get out much. They had a time picking people who weren't at least somewhat familiar with Samuel.

I take a seat by Angela Basset, the lawyer helping me present the case. Samuel's lawyer is one of his former frat brothers. They're pretty much the same person, except Lucas has even blonder hair and a silver watch instead of gold.

He has a great look for those personal injury lawyer billboards you see on the interstate.

Each lawyer stands and gives their opening statements. Angela holds her own against Lucas, highlighting all the crimes against our town and how Samuel used our business names and reputations to funnel money in and out of the bank for personal gain.

She mentions the evidence I have, from fake bank statements to wired conversations to the game-cam footage of him trying to manipulate Homer into joining him. She ends by bringing up that he might have intended to bring Homer in so he could pin it all on him. Lucas objects due to speculation. I take a deep breath as Angela sits down.

Lucas plays the small-town-bias angle, stating that everything is blown out of proportion because Samuel isn't from here. He continues to paint Samuel as someone misunderstood and manipulated by Ashley.

It takes all my restraint not to tackle him for that comment.

He smirks at me when he sits down. I slide my chair back the slightest bit, and Angela puts a hand on my arm to stop me.

I trust her and force myself to behave.

"I'd like to call Homer Giles to the stand," Lucas says.

Homer comes from the back of the room, dressed in a button-down flannel and new Carhartts. His hair is combed and slicked to the side. He is sworn in and sits beside the judge. Lucas leans in front of him, a devious smirk across his face.

He asks basic questions, trying to paint Homer as Samuel's only friend. That's probably not far from true, but

I'm not buying that as the reason Samuel tried to bring him in on the deal.

Homer remains surprisingly calm and answers every question brutally honestly bringing a few laughs at times. When Lucas grows tired of trying to belittle him, Angela stands for a cross-examination.

"Homer, how long have you banked at Smart Money Credit Union?"

"Oh gosh, since before it was that. Ever since I started working at the Pig as a grocery sacker in high school."

"So long before Samuel came?"

"Yes, ma'am." He nods and smooths a hand over his hair.

"So your business with the bank has no connection to knowing Samuel?"

Lucas tries to object on something stupid, but the judge overrules it this time.

"No, ma'am, I've always banked there."

Angela flashes me a confident look before she continues. She asks questions to prove that Samuel and Homer had a nonexistent relationship until recently, when Samuel came under suspicion and needed new businesses as cover-ups.

My blood pressure lowers when she excuses Homer and smiles my way. I glance at the jury. One older man is asleep, and a middle-aged woman is knitting. Seriously? At least the majority seem to care.

I'm called to present my findings from Homer's house, including the game cam and the recording. Some of the people laugh at my comments to Homer through the earpiece. Watching it for the first time without studying every aspect to pin Samuel, I can see the comedic effect.

Once I sit down, Lucas calls Paul to the stand. What a joke.

He gets little more out of him than how great the suckers taste. It's so uninformative that Angela doesn't care to cross-examine him. Instead, she has me present the evidence I found with Ashley to prove the "other businesses" Samuel mentioned to Homer.

I return to the front and set the projector to show all the documents Ashley managed to record with her phone. When I turn toward the crowd, I notice her in the back row. She must've snuck in during Paul's performance.

She gives me a tiny wave, and I smile slightly. That gives me a boost of adrenaline, and I present the documents and end with some photos that show the back-room setup at the bank.

Angela fist bumps me under the table when I return to my seat. Then she calls Ashley to the stand.

My palms sweat as I watch her walk up there. She makes eye contact with me after she's sworn in.

Angela has her introduce herself and her relationship to Samuel. When Ashley mentions they dated some in the past, I cringe. I still have nightmares about him kissing her when I was on the stakeout.

"Did Mr. Covington ever make you feel uncomfortable?"

Ashley lists the ways he belittled her while they dated and as an employee. Making her copy documents was just icing on the cake. It takes everything in me to not attack him right here in the courtroom.

"Did Sheriff Manning force you to go undercover?"

Ashley shakes her head and looks at me. "Not at all. He's the most respectful person I know. I've always had suspicions about Samuel and didn't like how he treated his employees, so I was happy to help."

"I see." Angela paces in front of the stand. "And what is your relationship to Sheriff Manning?"

"We've been friends for some time now, and I'm helping him with his campaign."

My heart aches at the friend zone, but I stuff my bruised feelings aside and refocus my goal on sticking it to Samuel.

"And do you think he asked you to run his campaign to get close to you so you'd help with the case?"

Ashley giggles, causing some of the crowd to snicker. "Not at all. The campaign was my idea. We did end up working on his campaign with the debate and all, but it was my idea first as a cover-up for why we were meeting about the case."

"No further questions."

Lucas stands before Ashley does. "I'd like to cross-examine, please."

The judge nods, and Lucas walks toward her. She squirms when he gives her the same pretty-boy smile Samuel does. Every nerve in my neck flares and I start to slide my chair again. Angela gives me a warning glance, and I simmer down.

We're so close to this being over. To Apple Cart being rid of Samuel.

"Miss Armstrong, is it true that you dated both Mr. Covington and Mr. Manning?"

"Objection!" Angela is the one to slide her chair back this time.

"Overruled." The judge motions for her to sit.

She plops down and crosses her arms. Ashley takes a deep breath before answering.

"No."

Whispers rise in the crowd. Judge Wright bangs his gavel. "Order."

They get silent quicker than a kid pinched for talking during altar call.

"Let me explain," Ashley continues. "I dated Samuel some in the past, but it was always rocky. He actually kissed me not long ago when I was at his house for dinner. I only went as part of the cover-up to see what he would say."

Samuel scowls at her.

"He's always been very handsy with me, which made for a weird work environment. In hindsight, I probably should've reported him, but his dad is the bank CEO and president. Plus, we have dated before. So the lines were a little blurred."

She sighs and looks at me. My limbs tingle. What will she say about me? I hope I never made her feel uncomfortable.

"As for Sheriff Manning, we didn't date because of the case. However, he is the kindest, most respectful man I've ever met outside of my immediate family. I have kissed him, but was never forced to. I wanted to kiss him as much or more than he wanted to kiss me. And if I weren't moving soon to take a new job, I would definitely date him, because I think I'm in love with him."

Ashley

"Order in the court."

My shoulders jerk at the judge's gavel banging. A few whispers linger as everyone ultimately obeys the "shush" order. I should've known such a candid confession would cause an uproar, but I did swear to tell the truth.

My gaze is still fixed on Bradley, who looks at me with a mixture of shock and admiration.

"No further questions." Samuel's lawyer sits down.

Every eye follows me as I walk to the back of the courtroom to claim my spot by the door. They stare at me until the judge bangs his gavel once more. He calls for each lawyer to give their closing argument.

Angela does a great job summarizing the evidence presented and mentioning how Samuel doesn't seem to have others' best interest in mind in any situation. That, I totally agree with.

Judge Wright dismisses the jury to deliberate and says we will reconvene after lunch. Bradley stands and handcuffs Samuel. One of his deputies comes from the crowd and helps him escort Samuel back to his cell for the deliberation period.

Samuel gives me a glance full of hatred when he passes through the courtroom doors. I halfway want to return the look, but decide he's getting plenty of payback already. Even on the off chance they say he is innocent—which he isn't—he's humiliated beyond measure. To him, that's probably worse than a criminal record.

The crowd funnels out of the room, and I hear my name among the chatter. Some of the older women stop by to say they hope it works out with Bradley and me.

What part of "I'm moving" do they not understand? Then I realize they likely forgot anything else after I said I'd date Bradley.

The last people out of the room are Samuel's parents. I dip my head, not wanting to face them. When his mom puts a hand on my shoulder, I don't know how to react.

"Ashley?" his dad asks.

"Yes, sir?" I slowly lift my head.

I haven't had much interaction with them. Only a few bank functions and one dinner at their house when Samuel and I officially dated for a bit.

"Can we talk?"

My body tries to go into flight mode, but there's nowhere to flee unless I run to the other end of the back bench. That would be weird and immature, so I stay. "Um . . ."

Mrs. Covington slides her hand away and sits on the bench in front of me. "Ashley, we're terribly sorry about Samuel. We apologize for his behavior and are very disappointed in him right now." I give her a sympathetic face. She pulls a tissue from her purse and blots the corners of her eyes.

Her husband motions for her to slide over and sits. He puts his arm around her for comfort, then looks at me. "We didn't raise him to act this way. He's being an entitled brat, and it caught up to him," Mr. Covington says.

I couldn't agree more, but fight the urge to shout "amen" at the top of my lungs.

He moves his arm from around his wife and leans closer. "We know he's guilty. The evidence is there, and we've heard him talk about sports betting."

"We had no idea he was funding it through the bank." Mrs. Covington sniffles.

"He should be ruled guilty," Mr. Covington continues. "By the slim chance he's not, I will not allow him to work at the bank again. He has to learn a lesson, and I have to keep the integrity of my company."

I nod. "I admire that."

He smiles. "And we admire you."

I wrinkle my forehead. This isn't making any sense.

"We know you're a hard worker and a smart girl. I've seen you interact with people from all branches and with customers. I know you mentioned moving, but I'd like to invite you to step into Samuel's role while we post his position."

I open my mouth, but nothing comes out.

"The board requires a job posting, but I hope you will

apply as well. You will have had bank management experience if you take the temp position."

Wow. Never in a million years did I expect this. I stare at my hands for a few seconds, not sure how to respond.

"I took a loan officer management job in Birmingham. I'm deciding on apartments now and start next Monday."

"I know that," he says. "This job will pay more, trust me."

"But you don't know my salary." I laugh.

"I don't need to. I'm willing to pay more for someone I and the people in this community trust to run the bank."

My jaw drops.

"Please consider it, dear." Mrs. Covington puts her hand on mine.

"Can I think about it for a day?"

"Of course." She pats my hand.

They stand and walk out as if that wasn't such a big deal. I guess it isn't to them, considering they have plenty of money and their son is about to go to jail.

I puff out my cheeks and slowly leave the courtroom. What a day this has been.

The courthouse is almost desolate. Everyone probably ran to Mary's to gossip about the trial during the break. I take a seat near the licensing window to process everything. I'm there maybe ten minutes when Angela rushes toward me from across the room.

"The judge said the jury has reached a verdict. Bradley is taking Samuel in there now."

My eyes widen. That was quick, which is either really good or really bad.

I follow her to the courtroom. The only people in the crowd are Samuel's parents, Vernon, and Paul sitting in the back row with a to-go box. With so many people still at lunch, I'm sure the rumors will be even stronger. It doesn't help that Paul is here. He's known way more for talking about matters than paying attention to them.

The jury comes in with the court clerk and take their seats. Samuel is seated with his lawyer. Bradley stands up front and calls the court to order. I sit a few rows behind him and Angela.

Judge Wright enters as if he's a headlining singer following the opening act. He smooths his robe and sits as well. "The jury has reached a verdict."

The court clerk walks to the front and opens a sheet of paper. Everyone stares with anticipation like she's about to announce who won the presidency.

"The jury finds him guilty."

She names off the charges, but I can't hear a thing. It's like I'm watching a soap opera on mute as I observe Samuel hanging his head and his mom crying. The gavel bangs, calling me back to attention. The judge sentences him to a state facility, causing his mom to cry harder. My heart aches for her.

Bradley handcuffs Samuel and escorts him out of the courtroom. His lawyer marches out in a rage, and his parents follow. I swallow hard when his mom sobs loudly. His dad puts an arm around her and leads her out.

Everyone watches them leave except Paul. He's busy eating whatever is in his box like he's at a dinner show rather than a trial.

Angela gathers her papers, and I stand to leave. Vernon catches me before I make it to the door. "Ashley, could you tell Bradley something for me?"

"Sure."

Or I hope so, at least. It all depends on his response to my undying love confession, but I don't say that.

"I'm dropping out of the race."

"But the election is next week."

He shrugs. "I know, but I didn't want this job anyway. I only wanted a pay raise and to better my career."

I blink. He sounds so sincere.

"Bradley is the best man for the job and deserves to keep it." He laughs. "Besides, I had to run on a Democrat ticket, and we know at least half of Apple Cart County votes straight Republican every election."

"That is true."

"Thanks to you both for running a good race, and congrats." He extends a hand.

I shake it and smile. "Thank you as well. We couldn't have asked for a better opposing candidate."

He turns and walks out, leaving me alone in the courtroom once again. Except for Paul sucking every possible piece of meat off a chicken wing.

I exit the courtroom for what I hope is the last time ever. Bradley comes from the opposite direction, without Samuel this time. He tips his hat and grins, then walks toward me. I smile uncontrollably, confident his smile is a good sign. He reaches me and puts his hands on my arms.

"So, what's this about you wanting to date me and thinking you're in love with me?" He rubs my arms and grins wider. Goose bumps swell under my sleeves and my face flushes. "I need to know if you're for real because I know I'm in love with you."

I blink. Bradley is in love with me? My heart beats so hard, I rest my hand on it to try and hold it still.

He pulls me closer with one hand and removes his hat with the other. Then he kisses me. Right there in the middle of the courthouse. Not quite as scandalous as a Baptist church elevator, but way more public.

I kiss him back, not caring who sees us. We're adults and we're in love. We can figure the details out later.

We only break apart when someone claps slowly behind

us. I turn my head to Paul with the to-go box squeaking under his arm as he claps. "Bravo. Wonderful show, Bradley. From defeating the villain to getting the girl."

Bradley bows, then Paul hurries away. We both burst out laughing.

And to think I wanted to move away from this place.

EPILOGUE

One Month Later

Bradley

"Surprise!" a bunch of off-key voices scream in my face.

I've barely opened Ashley's front door, and half the county stares back at me. I jump back and straighten my hat. "What's all this about?"

Trixie wags her tail with excitement as everyone smiles at me. Paul blows a party horn in my face, and Ms. Dot tosses confetti at me. I brush that off and look around for Ashley. This is her house, after all.

Actually, it's owned by the bank. And not in the sense of she owes on a loan, but in the sense that the Covingtons bought the house Samuel rented as a space for anyone managing the Apple Cart County branch. Currently, that job belongs to Ashley.

She shifts to the front of the crowd and hugs me. "Are you surprised?"

"Yeah. Where did everyone come from? Only your car is in the driveway."

Morgan swallows a bite of the sandwich she's munching on and raises her hand. "They parked in my yard to surprise you. I guess you didn't notice."

"To be honest, Morgan, you have so many kids and stuff in your yard, I didn't think anything of it."

She smiles at Ashley. "Told you he wouldn't."

Ashley bats her eyelashes at me, an excited look on her face. "This is an official party to celebrate your reelection."

I laugh, then turn from her to our friends. "I appreciate it and all, but the election was a month ago and Vernon dropped out."

"That don't make you any less our sheriff," Brother Johnny says. "Now if you want to eat all the delicious potluck we've prepared, I'll bless the food real quick."

He eyes Morgan, and she stops chewing. Funny how people around here obey the Baptist pastor more than the law. Or not funny, seeing as I'm the law.

I bow my head as he thanks God for the food and the fellowship of everyone in our community. A small county in Alabama might seem like a joke to some, but there's no place I'd rather be, and no people I'd rather protect.

"Amen." Brother Johnny breaks the prayer.

Everyone parts ways. Morgan grabs my arm and pulls me toward the kitchen. "You need to eat first. This is your party."

"Then why did you eat a sandwich already?"

She scoffs. "Someone has to test the food."

Ashley laughs and helps Morgan shove me through the crowd. Paul is halfway down the line with his to-go plate. I ignore him and grab a plate. Ashley falls in line behind me, then Morgan.

Maybe that's why she was so concerned about getting me to the food.

I'm glad the plates are the big rectangle kind so I can try some of everything. There's so much that I can't fit dessert on my plate. When I'm at the end of the line, I elbow Morgan. "Whistle for me."

She lets out her infamous whistle that can deafen dogs from a mile away. Trixie lies down in the corner and whines, proving my point. If rabbits have sensitive ears, Rambo is hurting about now too.

Ashley happily adopted him once Samuel went to jail. She couldn't bear putting him up for adoption, and the Covingtons didn't want a rabbit in their house.

Daisy offered to take him, but Ashley didn't want him mixed up in her zoo. Rabbit yoga isn't a thing, and the goats might play too roughly.

Every eye—and ear—turns to Morgan. I lift my hand to get their attention. "Thank y'all for doing this. I know I don't say it enough, but there's no place I'd rather live and serve than Apple Cart County."

A few people clap and many say thanks back to me. The chatter resumes and people crowd us to get food. I take Ashley's hand and lead her out the back door.

She sets her plate on the patio table and brushes her hands up her arms at the chill in the air.

"I can get you a blanket. I just needed room to eat." I set my plate beside hers and start in the house.

She grabs my hand. "Wait. I have some exciting news for us."

"Us?" I raise my brows.

"Yeah." She rubs her arms again.

I wrap her in a hug to keep her warm. Her eyes twinkle

as she gazes up at me. "I got the job."

"I know." I glance at the house. "That's why you're living here."

"No." She laughs. "The permanent job."

My mouth opens as I realize what she means.

The Covingtons posted Samuel's branch manager position and interviewed candidates while Ashley filled in. She was one of the candidates, but had to apply and interview like everyone else.

"Does this mean—"

She laughs and shakes her head. I pull her in and kiss her quickly, then pull back to admire her joyous face. "You're staying in Apple Cart for real."

"For real."

I smirk. "You know I would've still dated you long distance."

"Maybe."

"I would and you know it."

She shrugs. I frown.

"It doesn't matter because it all worked out," she says.

"Yeah, it's funny because here I was thinking I'd never have a girl I like move to Apple Cart."

She laughs. "I only lived in Sparrow."

"You know, a wise man once told me that sometimes you have to go outside the county to find what you're really looking for."

She wrinkles her forehead. "Let me guess. Paul said that about junk."

"Nope. Roy about chicken gizzards."

We laugh and share another kiss as I pull her in tighter. Things really did all work out.

ACKNOWLEDGMENTS

First, I'd like to thank God for giving me creative ideas and placing the right people in my path to help see them to fruition.

My husband, Blake, gets credit next for always supporting my writing endeavors, even if he finds my stories a little too "girly."

I also want to thank my readers and ARC team for their support. You. Are. Awesome! I could not do what I do without my readers and support team. I love y'all!

As always, I'd like to thank my editor, Joanne, and my proofreader, Charity. Both of these ladies are huge help to making my books shine!

ABOUT THE AUTHOR

Kaci Lane is a journalist turned fiction writer who believes all stories should have a happy ending. While unsuccessfully trying to learn Spanish for a decade, she has become fluent in sarcasm, Southern belle and movie quotes. She is married to a Southern Gentleman and has two young children who help keep her humility in check. Connect with her on kacilane.com or check out kacilanebooks.com for more books.

BOOKS BY KACI LANE

Bama Boys Series

Hunting for Love

Chicken about Love

Hammered by Love

Cutting out Love

Geared for Love

Apple Cart County Christmas Series

Christmas in Dixie

Crazy Rich Rednecks

Queen of my Double-Wide Trailer

Single Southern Mamas Series

Mom Squad

Mom Ball

Schooled on Love Series

Taco Truck Takedown

Side Hustle

Buggy List

Off-Season

Books in Shared Series with Other Authors

No Time for Traditions

A Perfect Match in Silver Leaf Falls

Brewin' Up Love
Baking Spirits Bright

www.ingramcontent.com/pod-product-compliance
Lightning Source LLC
LaVergne TN
LVHW041801060526
838201LV00046B/1082